Shadows the Sizes of Cities

A Novel

GREGORY W. BEAUBIEN

MORESBY PRESS

Published by Moresby Press, LLC, Chicago

www.moresbypress.com

Copyright © 2014 by Gregory W. Beaubien

First Printing

Book design by Suzanne Griffin

ISBN 978-0-9911816-0-5

For Patricia

PART I

Chapter One

O N THE DAY THAT EVERYTHING CHANGED I stood on the deck of the ferry in the windy sun and watched the gray cliffs come into view. Farther down the coast there were green hills and flat white buildings jumbled over the rises, with minarets standing into the cool blue sky. The ferry docked at the base of the hills where several vessels were moored in the water and the sun shone on a rust-colored freighter off to our left. I thought about the man who'd knocked me down and robbed me, and about the Dutchman's offer—so much now that the thoughts shoved and screamed against each other inside my skull and pushed out against its edges. I doubted I could go through with it. I was broke and pissed off, but I wasn't a bad person.

My companions, of course, had no idea what was going on. Tammy was in a good mood, chattering with Nigel and pushing her blond hair away from her eyes. When we bounded down the gangplank with our bags I felt the metal swaying under my feet. In the arrival terminal the guides immediately surrounded us.

"*Guten tag, wie geht's?*"

"I'm not German."

"American? Need taxi?"

The teenage boy was wearing a shiny brown polyester

shirt. He smiled at me.

"No, thanks."

"I give you good tour of Kasbah and medina. Best in town."

Several others followed alongside us, throwing pitches. Marissa stayed close to me. Outside there were taxis and buses and a single pair of railroad tracks that ended inside a shed at the end of the wharf to our right.

"You looking for train station?"

"Yes."

"It is right this way," the boy said, pointing to the little building at the end of the track. "I will take you there."

Marissa and Tammy looked at me uneasily. Nigel was behind Tammy.

"I happen to know that the train station is in the opposite direction," I said, pointing toward the town.

"Yes," the boy replied, bowing his head. "But may I show you the medina?"

I laughed. "No, thanks, we don't need any help." We started toward the esplanade.

"You are no better than a woman!" the guide yelled, spitting on the ground.

Marissa stopped and turned toward him, sun reflecting off her short dark hair. I grabbed her arm. "Don't say anything. Just keep walking."

"Creep."

We passed the turnoff for the road that zigzagged up the side of the hill to the ancient town above it. From the markets along the inclining street music drifted down in shrill semitones, nagging repetitions on a Moroccan clarinet. Ahead of us between the lanes of traffic on the boulevard a strip of park was landscaped with palm trees and flowers and there was a footpath through the grass with benches where people were sitting. Hotels and cafés faced across the median toward the bay. Signs were in French and Arabic. The buildings were all white and three or four stories high, with French architecture and wrought-iron Juliet balconies. Men sitting in the cafés gave us cold stares.

In the train station a few dozen passengers were sitting on their luggage waiting to depart, their strange guttural language echoing through the round terminal. Barefoot country women in white straw hats with strands of dark yarn connecting the crowns and rims sat on the floor, stout legs splayed in front of them, next to burlap sacks of fruits and vegetables. The women wore coarse white cloth and had designs tattooed on their foreheads and hands. The soles of their bare feet were black and swollen.

Looking around the station I saw a pair of young men staring at us. Unlike the others who wore traditional clothing these two were attired in slacks and dress shirts. My companions didn't seem to notice them.

"Let's see what time the next train leaves for Rabat," Nigel said.

"Three o'clock."

"How do you know that?"

"Read it in the guidebook."

"Aye, there's your man."

At the ticket counter Nigel spoke French with the teller, who sat looking bored on the other side of the vertical bars.

Tammy and I moved closer around Nigel as he dug into the pouch around his wrist and removed a roll of bills. We bought our tickets and then walked and sat on our bags closer to the open doors to the track platform. Tammy gasped. A beggar was crouching on the floor crying as a policeman repeatedly struck his head and shoulders with a black truncheon, the blows landing with cracks and thuds.

"That poor man," Tammy whispered. "Being hit on the head is my worst fear."

In the even light her green irises were sharply beautiful and the skin on her face was moist and smooth. I tried to re-assure her with my expression, pleased that she had turned to me. Over her shoulder I saw the two young men staring at us.

"I'm thirsty as hell," Marissa said, looking around the room. "Can we get something to drink?"

"I'll find some sodas."

Deliberately I made eye contact with the thinner of the two, giving him a hard look. He stared back at me blank-ly. There was a snack counter near the ticket window and I bought four cans of Coke and a bottle of mineral water. Looking back I chuckled at the sight of my companions, the only foreigners in the station and dressed absurdly: Nigel pale and gaunt with his long black hair and sunken cheeks, a white collared shirt hanging out of his black jeans; Tammy in Doc Martens, tomboy jeans and a black zippered jacket; Marissa, pea-green headscarf and black stretch pants, toes and ankles bare through the straps of black sandals.

They were quiet as we sat sipping our drinks and waiting for the train. The two young men continued watching us, but it still seemed that I was the only one in our group who noticed them. I didn't say anything to the others. Several times I caught the thin one staring at Tammy or me. He was shorter than the other, with a moustache and wavy hair. Of the two, his face seemed the more intelligent, as if complex thoughts were churning behind his dark eyes. He glanced at us while he smoked a cigarette. I tried not to look at him.

"Le cabinet, s'il vous plait?"

The porter pointed toward the platform outside and crooked his finger to the left. On my way out I passed the thin stranger. Our eyes met again, much closer this time.

I stepped outside onto the platform. Beyond the tracks there was an empty lot and then storage sheds and cranes near the port. In the lavatory a man with thin brown limbs was crouching in his underwear, washing himself from a bucket. I stood and pissed through a little hole in the floor. On the other side of a partial divider a man squatted with his back toward the wall. The smell choked my throat.

Outside a muezzin's cry rose from a minaret somewhere in the town, a moaning ascension at once peaceful and ominous. The notes sustained and then fell, in lonely, winding half-steps. The man who had been washing himself was now on the train platform, kowtowing on a mat and pleading with the sky. I wondered what he was hoping for and whether he would ever get it.

Tammy, Nigel and Marissa were also outside. Nigel was holding my duffel bag.

"What's going on?"

"The train is due in ten minutes," he said.

"We'll probably have a compartment to ourselves."

I looked around for the sharp dressers but didn't see them. The country women had lugged their sacks onto the platform and now stood with the rest of the crowd waiting for the train. An old man in a skullcap buttoned his brown robe and peered down the tracks.

When the train rolled into the station we found the car and climbed aboard. Our compartment was the first one on the end, on the side facing the station. I tossed my bag onto the upper rack and then did the same for Marissa and Tammy. The compartment had six seats, three facing three, and I sat by the window with a reverse view. Marissa sat beside me, and Tammy and Nigel were across from us.

I wasn't surprised to see the two young strangers appear in the doorway. "Are these taken?" the thin face asked in perfect English, gesturing toward the two empty seats by the door.

"Please," Nigel said, "come in."

The larger of the two said nothing as he walked in behind the other, beaming a squinty smile and nodding his head as he took the seat next to Marissa. His friend sat across from him, next to Nigel. They were carrying only light bags, which they placed on the floor by their feet.

My companions enthusiastically began introducing themselves to the strangers. I turned to look out the window.

"My name is Fareed," the thin face said. "And this is my cousin, Adir."

"I'm Nigel, this is Tammy, Marissa and Will."

They took turns reaching across the small space to shake hands. I was last.

"I just arrived from London," Fareed announced, turning to look at Tammy and Nigel. Their faces lit up.

"Oh, I love London!" Tammy cried, smiling at Fareed and leaning across Nigel toward him.

"I study at a small college there," Fareed continued. "Computers. My cousin met me at the airport and now we're going home to our village, just down the coast from here." Adir smiled and nodded. "Have you been to Morocco before?" Fareed asked.

The train jerked into motion. "No, this is our first time," Tammy said.

"Where are you headed?"

"To Rabat," Nigel told him. "And then on from there."

The platform began to recede and then the station, opening a view of the palm trees and low white buildings along the boulevard. Taxis climbed the road up the side of the gray rock toward the medina. Above it white cubes crowded over the hills and the mountain of Tangier rose in the background. Soon we were rolling across a plateau of scrubby, pale-green pasture. A shepherd carrying a staff walked with his flock. The Atlantic glinted in the distance.

None of my companions was noticing the sights. They

leaned toward the strangers in eager conversation.

"You're American?" Fareed asked, looking at Tammy.

"Well, the three of us are," she said, pointing to Marissa and me.

"But not you?" Fareed looked at Nigel.

"No, no, *Irlandais*. From Ireland."

"Have you been to the U.S.?" Marissa asked.

"Not yet."

"Well if you do, you *have* to come to Chicago."

"Oh, absolutely!" Tammy said. "We could show you around!"

Fareed nodded politely. "But why are you going to Rabat?"

"What do you mean?" Marissa said.

"There is nothing in Rabat," Fareed said, frowning and shaking his head. "You should come to our village instead."

Tammy chuckled.

"We live in a beautiful town by the sea. And you are in luck. There is a festival, tonight only. We will be your hosts."

"Really?" I said. "Tonight only?"

Tammy gave me an annoyed glance and Fareed looked at me guardedly. "Yes, there is a big festival tonight. You should not miss it."

"Nah, mate," Nigel said. "We're heading on to Rabat, but thank you, anyway."

"But it takes five hours to reach Rabat!" Fareed persisted. "The train will arrive in our village in forty minutes, in time to watch the sun set over the sea!"

I could tell by their faces that Tammy and Marissa were considering the stranger's suggestion. "Well, that's a very nice offer," I told him, "but we've already paid for our tickets to Rabat."

"There is no problem," Fareed said. "You can get back on board tomorrow with the same tickets and go to Rabat."

"Really?!" Tammy grinned at him. I tried to make eye contact with her but she was still looking at Fareed.

"My aunt has a pensión in the medina," he went on. "You can stay there very cheap, in a traditional Moroccan house. We will show you a good restaurant for dinner, with the best fish, fresh from the sea."

Tammy looked at Nigel and smiled, raising her eyebrows and biting her lower lip.

"Sounds great to me," Marissa said.

"Tammy," I said with an edge in my voice, "I really think we should stay on the train to Rabat. You know they're expecting us."

I finally had her attention and she looked at me, rolled her eyes and turned away. Tammy was accustomed to her role as queen bee of her business and social circles, the arbiter who set the rules and made the decisions for others to follow. The fact that her ideas were often foolish didn't seem to matter. She was ignorant and not very bright and yet supremely self-confident, to the edge of hubris. During the epic parties that she threw at her huge apartment in Wicker Park people were drawn to her because she was cute and charismatic and energetic and fun. She laughed a lot and had that special allure that rich girls often have. Even with the punkish clothes she'd been wearing lately you could see old family money in her posture and on her face, in the confident way that she carried herself. Despite the differences in our backgrounds and her self-righteous attitude I had always liked her on a one-to-one basis. But I didn't want any part of the group mentality that Tammy had built around herself.

"No, I think we should see the fishing village," Nigel said decisively, still looking at her. "Sounds brilliant." Tammy screeched with delight.

"Excuse me."

I rose to my feet and squeezed past their knees, sliding

the door closed behind me. The train bounced rhythmically as I walked down the corridor past the windows. Sunlight illuminated the pastureland and the high green edges of the Rif Mountains in the distance. I thought Tammy might follow me out. She did not.

As I walked back to the compartment I could hear them through the door, laughing. Tammy's nasal snort was loudest of all. She glanced up at me as I walked in, but then quickly turned her eyes back to the strangers.

"We spent a month in Mexico, and one day Nigey was trying to order eggs in a restaurant," she said, giggling. "But neither of us could speak Spanish, and the waiter didn't speak any English. So, Nigey gets up," she stood in the cramped space of the train, "and starts moving around like a chicken!" Tammy bent her knees and waved her elbows at her sides. Marissa squealed with laughter.

I had to maneuver past the legs of the others and as I sat by the window I noticed the expression on Fareed's face. He was smiling at Tammy's charade but I saw contempt in his eyes. His cousin continued his obsequious grinning.

"Are we almost there?" Tammy asked, looking out the window for the first time since we had left Tangier.

"Five more minutes," Fareed said.

"Tammy," I said, hearing my own hard flat voice, "I don't think we should get off this train before Rabat. I mean it."

"Oh, for God's sake, Will, don't be so rude!" Marissa snapped. "These people are trying to show us their hospitality!"

"Yeah, Will, what's your problem?" Tammy's tone was that of a disappointed mother scolding her misbehaving child.

"I cannot *wait* to see this town," Marissa chirped, squirming in her seat and smiling at Fareed.

I turned to look out the window. The sun was silver on the ocean and fishing boats floated in black silhouette against the water. I wondered what my father would have thought of my travel companions. Hell, I knew exactly what he would have thought. What he would think of the plan I was considering was another matter. The idea made me feel sick.

Soon Fareed was smiling and pointing out the window. "Here we are!"

A glimpse of the town flashed by and then was blocked by the station as the train came to a stop. I handed Tammy and Marissa their bags. Fareed and Adir left the compartment first, followed by Marissa and Nigel. I wrapped my fingers around Tammy's elbow and whispered in her ear.

"You know these guys are hustlers, don't you? I've read about these kinds of scams."

"You're paranoid, Will, and you're getting on my nerves." She grimaced and pulled away from me.

"You're making a mistake."

"Oh, well. I guess we're going to find out." She turned her back to me and left the compartment.

My choices were to follow them or continue on the train alone. I thought again about the stranger and the Dutchman's offer. The way I saw it, Tammy had helped make my decision for me. At least I had tried to warn her. When I stepped off the car she was already a few yards ahead of me with the others.

Chapter Two

Between the train station and the ramparts of the town a plaza was gray with pebbles. They crunched under my shoes as I stepped quickly to bring myself alongside Fareed. I had decided to play along, for now.

"Were you born here?"

He jumped as he turned to look at me. "Yes, I've lived here all my life, except for my time in London."

"You speak English very well."

"Most of the young people here speak Arabic, French, Spanish and English. Some Italian and German, too."

"Most Americans can barely speak English," I said, chuckling and shaking my head. His expression told me that he didn't understand what I meant.

"There is a café on the beach where we will take you after dinner," Fareed said, pointing to a thatched-roof structure facing the water. "We will drink tea and smoke hashish." He looked at me, gauging my reaction.

"Yeah, all right," I said.

Tammy, Nigel and Marissa had been walking with Adir behind Fareed and me. I paused to let them catch up.

"This wall was built by the Portuguese, in the fifteenth century," Fareed said, proudly pointing to the brown ramparts surrounding the village.

The rock wall was three stories high and ten feet thick. We passed through the shade of its bulbous Moorish entry-way into the medina. Narrow pathways splintered between high white-stucco walls.

"Ooo, look at this place!" Tammy said, smiling and hunching her shoulders as she walked along holding Nigel's hand.

"It's wonderful," Marissa said, looking around wide-eyed.

The buildings were white boxes with flat facades connected in long series by the walls that obscured whatever lay on the other side. There might be a house or a garden or a tiled courtyard with a fountain, but from the street you saw only the blank, inscrutable white wall, ten feet from an identical barrier running parallel to it on the other side of the alley. There were no windows, only doors of heavy wood or studded metal, some shut, others open to shops inside, often with a man standing in the frame. Along some stretches horizontal blue stripes were painted across the lower halves of the walls. The crooked streets were paved with stones and far too narrow for cars to pass. Women covered in *haiks* hurried along with children and bags of produce while men loitered in the doorways and cafés, watching us with their chins lowered toward their chests. The air smelled of the sea and I could hear waves hitting the rocks below the ramparts.

Fareed and Adir led us through a jumble of alleys to a small house on a corner. "When you greet someone," Fareed said, stopping in front of a sky-blue door, "you must place your right hand over your heart and say, '*Salam aleikoom.*'"

We practiced the greeting while Adir turned a key in the door, opening it into a dim space. Adir and Fareed walked in first, followed by Tammy and Nigel and then Marissa and me. I glanced up the street before stepping inside—two men were watching us from a nearby doorway. One of them looked at me and shook his head.

Inside the house there was a small foyer and then an

empty space with a high ceiling and a flight of steps leading up to the second floor. A bathroom was wedged beneath
the stairs; the door was open and I could see white tiles on
the floor. The steps had no balustrade and they climbed one
wall and then turned and continued up the perpendicular
side to a door at the top. Next to the door at a ninety-degree
angle there was another door that was open to a tiny room.
Fareed stopped to introduce us to an old couple standing
inside; an amber lamp on a low table shone up toward their
faces, throwing moving shadows across the ceiling.

"Salam aleikoom," I said, bowing slightly and placing my
right hand over my heart.

The old couple repeated the gesture, smiling awkwardly.

"Each room costs forty dirhams for the night," Fareed
told us.

Nigel tried to turn his back as he took money from the
pouch. He handed the notes to the old man. "Merci, monsieur."

We followed Fareed through the other door into an unfinished space, a large empty area with a low ceiling and a
concrete floor covered with powdery dust. In the dim light
I noticed two brown paper bags of cement mix on the floor
along the far wall. To the left a short flight of wooden steps
led up to the roof.

"Two people can sleep in here," Fareed said, opening a
door to the right.

We stepped into a small square room with no windows.
The white walls were blank and there were benches along
three of them, padded with red cushions.

"Nigey and I call this one!" Tammy cried, tossing her bags
onto one of the benches.

"I will show you the other room," Fareed said, leading Marissa and me out the door and turning to the right through
the unfinished space.

Adir stood in the background and watched. There were holes cut in the rear wall, W-shaped and low to the floor, and through them I glimpsed the flat rooftops of the adjacent houses, all jumbled together, a chaotic dream. Marissa was ahead of me and as Fareed opened the door to the second bedroom I heard her cry out happily. Inside there was a bed made with sheets, blankets and pillows. Marissa looked at me with a naughty smile and bounced on the edge of the bed.

"Are you hungry?" Fareed asked us.

"Sure."

"We will take you to eat the best seafood in Morocco."

Everyone's spirits seemed high as we strolled through the streets, liberated from the burden of our bags. The town was picturesque and uncrowded. I inhaled the fresh sea air.

Walking back through the gate we followed Fareed along the edge of the plaza to a restaurant at the base of the ramparts. The little white building had café seating.

"Great!" Tammy said. "We can eat outside!"

"The service is better inside," Fareed said seriously.

Tammy's smile fell. "Well, all right…."

The proprietor was a smiling man in a blue djellaba with gray stripes. He showed us to a long table and handed us menus. Fareed sat at the head of the table and I took a chair at the end to his left. Nigel sat across from me, next to Tammy and Adir. Marissa sat beside me.

"Can we get a beer, then?"

Fareed looked at Nigel. "Alcohol is forbidden."

"Really, even for tourists?"

"That's all right," I said. "Let's just order a couple big bottles of mineral water. With gas or without?"

The waiter set plates of salad on the table. "We probably shouldn't eat this," I said quietly to Tammy.

"No, I'm sure it's all right." She looked down at the floor.

"Why do tourists talk only about the bad things in our country?" Fareed asked, frowning. "They go home and say that the food makes them sick, that the people are poor and illiterate. I hope you will tell the Americans about the good things here."

"Of course."

Out the window I could see a group of men sitting at the café tables, watching people pass through the square. Fareed noticed me looking at them.

"Their wives do all the work."

Marissa huffed.

"Is it true that the men can have three wives?" I asked.

"Yes," Fareed said. "But only one heart."

We followed his recommendation and ordered fresh fish, grilled and served with rice and vegetables. When the plates arrived we sat eating in awkward silence. But the fish was good and it revived me.

After a few minutes Fareed said: "How long will you be in Morocco?"

"Three weeks," Nigel said, sitting up straight.

"What are your plans?"

"We're not sure yet," I said quickly.

Nigel looked at me. "No, but we have a general plan. On to Rabat for a night, and then to Marrakesh. Perhaps the Sahara."

I glared at him. "But as you saw today, we don't always stick to our plans."

"Spontaneity keeps things interesting," Tammy said, looking at me irritably.

"Absolutely," Marissa agreed.

When we had finished dinner Fareed excused himself. I saw him walk to the back of the restaurant, where he made a call from a French payphone on a countertop. We offered to pay for the dinner and our hosts accepted. A few minutes later the six of us were walking back through the medina.

"So where's the big festival?" I asked.

"We will take you to see traditional Moroccan handicrafts," Fareed said. He pointed to a man passing us in the narrow lane, draped in a long gauzy white robe with gold piping. "You should buy a djellaba like this one," Fareed told us, "and wear it while you are in Morocco. No one will bother you."

Marissa was walking ahead of me, alongside Tammy. I heard her saying she wanted to skip the festival. "I'm just so beat, I wouldn't enjoy it. I'd rather go back to the pensión and lie down."

Tammy's voice sounded strained as she forced herself to agree with Marissa. "I thought the festival was the whole reason we came here… but okay, if that's what you want to do. We'll all stop back at the pensión for a minute and drop you off."

When we reached the thick blue door Adir waited in the street while Fareed took us upstairs. The space was dark and empty and we climbed the steps along the walls. At the upper landing I walked with Marissa through the unfinished addition to the rear bedroom.

"Are you sure you don't want to come with us?"

"I didn't sleep last night and I'm completely exhausted," she said, falling back onto the bed.

"Me too, but I'm starting to get a second wind. This could be a once-in-a-lifetime opportunity. Come with us to the festival. Afterwards we'll smoke in the café on the beach and then we can get some sleep."

"No, I'm staying here."

I lowered my voice to a whisper. "Marissa, I don't think it's safe for you to be here alone. I don't trust these people."

She rolled her eyes. "Stop trying to be my protector, Will.

I can take care of myself."

Just then I heard Tammy's voice behind us. "C'mon, let's go, man!"

"All right, then. See you later, Marissa."

Tammy, Nigel, Fareed and I went down the steps to the first floor. I stopped to use the bathroom under the stairs, ducking through the low door of the wedge-shaped space. There was a squat-hole toilet on the floor under the sharp corner. The wider side of the room had a spigot mounted on the wall with a little rubber hose and a bucket. I washed my hands and looked at my reflection in the tiny mirror. My face was sunburned and lack of sleep hung under my eyes.

When I stepped back into the foyer the others were already outside in the street. Adir stood there holding the door open and waiting for me, still wearing the same obsequious smile.

Fareed led us through the labyrinthine alleys of the town. The sun had moved lower over the Atlantic and the streets were dark in shadow on one side. Electric lights were starting to glow in the shop doorways. A muezzin's cry ascended in swelling, sustained tones. A chill slipped into the breeze.

The festival that Fareed had promised turned out to be nothing more than a visit to a carpet shop, a standard hustle that I had read about months earlier. I was on guard but played along. Tammy and Nigel offered no acknowledgment that they had been duped, and I did nothing to seek one from them.

"Aye, there's your man."

The shop owner was standing in the doorway, wearing a djellaba. He did not speak English.

"Salam aleikoom," we said, adroit hands over our hearts.

The middle-aged man nodded and smiled, repeating our gesture. As we stepped into a room with carpets covering the walls and floors a young boy brought out a silver tray with a pot of mint tea and six glasses. He lifted the spout of the ornately patterned tin pot two feet above the little glasses as he poured. Steam rose from the long cascade.

"To cool the tea," Fareed said.

The glasses had no handles and were hot to touch. The man showed us how to hold them, thumb on top, forefinger on the bottom. Tammy looked at me uneasily and I winked at her as we sipped the tea. The shop owner began pointing out the rugs. I glanced over to make sure I could still see the door.

"They are all handmade, of wool," Fareed told us. "These rugs will last for one hundred years."

"How much is this one?" Tammy asked, pointing at a huge rug patterned in blues and reds that hung on the wall beside her.

Fareed spoke to the man in Moghrebi, the Moroccan Arabic. "He says it is worth three thousand dollars, but you can name your price."

"Oh, that's all right!" Tammy giggled. "It would be too heavy for me to carry, anyway!"

"He can ship it anywhere in the world for you," Fareed persisted. "In America you can sell this rug for twice that much."

"Maybe on our way back north, in a couple of weeks."

Fareed looked at Tammy disdainfully. "You will not find rugs like this anywhere else in Morocco."

"I'm sorry," she said. "But no."

In the rear of the shop the man led us up a narrow staircase built of raw lumber against the side of a gray wall. On the second floor we brushed between rows of carpets hanging from the ceiling. Sandalwood incense was burning and an Egyptian pop song whined from a transistor radio.

We reached a clearing in the rugs where woodcarvings

and other knickknacks were arranged on shelves. I picked up a little round box. The lid came off with a soft pop. The cedar aroma was strong and sweet. I set it back down next to a round container made of pressed tin, with a star design on the top.

Fareed pushed Nigel and me to buy djellabas.

"They're lovely, lovely," Nigel told him. "But I'd better conserve me shillings, mate. So thank you, no."

Fareed was sulky as we left the shop and walked through the medina. Men in the doorways cast baleful eyes at us. We followed the cousins back to the plaza outside the rampart wall, across the crunchy gravel to the café on the beach. The sun was a swollen orange ball above the black horizon of the sea, throwing its color over the dark waves. Fareed led us to a table facing the water; I glanced around and saw that Tammy was the only woman there. The tall shiny blonde could hardly have been more conspicuous among the group of Arab men quietly smoking in the café. Music played low. A breeze was blowing off the water, laced with the sweet aroma of hashish. I zipped up my jacket.

The waiter brought mint tea. Fareed rolled a cigarette with tobacco and clumps of blond hashish, which he lit and passed around. When it came to me I drew on the cigarette slowly and luxuriously, stretching back in my chair and watching the tremulous orange fire melt into the black water. Silhouettes of the fishing boats bobbed against the light and I could hear them clanging. I opened my mouth and let the smoke roll out. A Moroccan seated at a nearby table nodded to me and smiled, holding up his thin hashish pipe. I nodded back. A little boy about eight years old sat beside the man, looking up at him with wonder.

As the cigarette went around our host's mood suddenly improved. "Teach me some American slang," Fareed said.

"Like what?"

"The things Americans say. 'Make like a tree and leave.'"

Tammy's laugh honked through the café.

"Make like a banana and split."

"What?!"

"No, not like that!"

"Wait—"

We all broke out laughing.

Another young Moroccan appeared at our table.

"This is our friend, Mahmoud."

I almost didn't notice that Adir had quietly stood and left the café. We watched the sun sink into the Atlantic. I was tired but felt relaxed and contented, forgetting everything for a few minutes. Staring at the water I was only vaguely aware of Nigel whispering to Fareed and Mahmoud: *"Just a tiny bit for later, mates…."*

When we left the café Mahmoud walked back with us through the maze of the medina, now ink black in the night. Even the white stucco walls seemed murky. In some places the streets were only six feet wide, with walls rising fifteen feet high on either side. A man standing on another man's shoulders could not reach the top. Some of the alleys ended in a T-shape at a wall, with paths bending left and right. The streets were so narrow that when we passed men they were just inches from us but in the darkness their eyes were still blurred. With the night chill many of them had raised the pointed hoods on their djellabas, further obscuring their faces. Electric light inside the shops cast the men in the doorways in silhouette.

Our group was quiet. Even Tammy said nothing as we stumbled through the dark. The sound of our footfalls echoed between the walls. Following Fareed and Mahmoud we turned and came upon a group of young men standing at a corner where black alleys bent crookedly away in four directions. At first I didn't see them in the darkness, even as they stood five feet in front of us. Their eyes were in shadow but as someone lit a cigarette I got a good look at the one in front; there was a purple birthmark on his cheek. I expected them to jump us right then. But as we walked past they only stared.

Chapter Three

WHEN WE RETURNED to the house I opened the bedroom door to find Marissa sitting up in the bed, looking anxiously at me.

"What's going on?"

"Fareed brought another friend and we're going to hang out in the other room for a while."

"How was the festival?"

"There was no festival. They just took us to a carpet shop."

She looked at me with surprise, but like Tammy and Nigel she ignored the fact that I had been right to mistrust the strangers. I told myself that whatever happened next would serve them right.

"Did you go to the café on the beach?"

"Yeah."

"How was it?"

"It was nice. We had a smoke and watched the sunset over the water. How about you? Been sleeping?"

Marissa pulled the sheets to one side. She was wearing just a tank top and panties. The skin was smooth on her legs and shoulders.

"No," she said. "I've been laying here crying, regretting that I didn't go with you."

I was taken aback. "Why?"

"I kept thinking about what you said—that I shouldn't miss that once-in-a-lifetime chance."

"Oh, don't worry. You didn't miss much. C'mon, let's go to the other room. Unless you're too tired."

I could see the relief she was feeling. "I'll hang out for a while," she said.

As Marissa pulled on her jeans and chunky-heeled sandals I glanced at the rumpled sheets on the bed. She looked at me with a lusty smirk.

The other room was already filled with smoke. Strata hung in motionless air, defined in the glow of a single bare light bulb suspended on a cord from the ceiling. Tammy and Nigel were sitting on the bench along the rear wall, giggling. They had sunburned faces and bloodshot eyes. I was surprised to see Adir sitting by the door. Fareed was next to him. Mahmoud sat on the other side.

"This is Marissa," I said as we entered the little room.

She said hello and placed her hand over her heart. Mahmoud looked at the floor and said nothing.

I sat beside Tammy. There was still a little room on the bench to my right.

"You can sit here, Marissa."

"No, that's all right," she said, squatting next to the door. "I'm fine here."

Tammy knelt down and handed the burning cigarette to Marissa.

When the joint came to me I held up my palm. "No, thanks. I've had enough." I looked at my watch and saw it was eleven-fifteen. "Twenty-four hours ago, we were in Madrid. We've barely slept since then."

Our hosts were silent and morose. They stared at the floor. Fareed seemed nervous. Tammy was oblivious to the change in them and went on jabbering with Nigel and Marissa.

Mahmoud still had not said a word. And then he suddenly

opened a leather bag and removed what looked like a loaf of bread wrapped in aluminum foil.

"You will buy this now," Fareed announced, looking at me.

"What the hell is it?"

Mahmoud peeled back the foil to reveal the largest piece of hashish I had ever seen. It was dark brown with the texture of lightly burnt pie crust.

"Holy shit," Tammy said.

"My God," said Nigel. "I've never seen anything like that before in my life!"

"You wanted to buy hashish, and here it is," Fareed said. "One thousand U.S. dollars. Right now."

The color blanched from Nigel's face. Marissa looked at me, scared.

"No way, man," I said. "We don't want that much. Just a little bit for later, a couple grams." I smiled at them.

"We do not sell just a couple of grams," Mahmoud said.

"Well, this is way too much. What would we do with all of this?"

"You can sell it," Fareed said impatiently. "Take it to Spain, double your money."

I listened to my heart beating in my temples. "Maybe we could just cut off a small piece?"

Mahmoud looked at me. "How much?"

I drew my finger down the side of the brick, about an inch from the end.

Mahmoud had a pocketknife and he began hacking through the thick, resinous hashish. The piece he cut off looked like the heel on a loaf of bread. He handed it to me. "Two hundred dollars."

"That's still too much."

"The people we got this from will not tolerate anything less!" Fareed said, raising his voice. "You must buy it now, two hundred dollars!"

Mahmoud pouted as he sat holding the remainder of the kilo, rubbing his thumb against the cut. "No," he said. "I cannot give it back to them like this. You must buy the whole thing. One thousand dollars!"

"Sorry, my friend, but that's impossible."

"If you do not buy this right now, there will be trouble with the police," Fareed said, looking at me. "You will go to jail, and your embassy will not help you. It will be very bad for your women. Very bad."

I touched Tammy's arm. "Why don't you and Marissa go wait for us in the other room?"

"No, we'll stay here."

I looked at her. "Go into the other room and wait for us. Do it now."

"Take out your money!" Adir yelled, his face contorted with hatred. "I want a hundred extra for showing you this town."

Nigel was pale. He sat trembling on the bench, chewing his fingertips. "J-J-Just a minute, mate, just give us a minute, please."

"Goddamn it, Tammy," I said, louder than before. "Go with Marissa and wait in the other room."

"Yes, go," Nigel said to her, his voice cracking.

As Tammy stood and began walking toward the door, Adir jumped up and grabbed her from behind, locking his elbow around her neck.

"Nigel!"

Tammy's boyfriend looked at her in terror but didn't move from the bench.

"We do not work for free!" Adir bellowed at me. He had his right arm around her neck and the palm of his other hand against the left side of her head. "Now take out your money, you son of a dog, or I will break this whore's neck!"

Fareed was sitting diagonally from me on my left. "Do what

he says," he told me. "Do it now."

Marissa was still on the floor near the door, looking up at Tammy and Adir with terror in her bloodshot eyes. My mouth was dry and my heart was pounding. As Adir held Tammy he began grinding his pelvis against her backside. She let out a long, groaning sob. Fareed sprang to his feet and came at me. Though I had not been there and possessed only an imagined memory of the event, an image of my father's shooting nonetheless existed sharply in my mind, and now it flashed through my consciousness. The woman's husband had broken her nose and blood was running into her mouth as she leveled the revolver at him. The neighbors heard yelling and called 911. When my father entered the kitchen the woman jumped with fear and turned and fired; his body jerked with the ringing bang. The air smelled of burnt gunpowder, an acrid metal death smell. The anguish and the anger that burned from the terrible understanding that strangers had shattered my life now surged through me again. I was barely aware of standing and before I could think the switchblade was out of my pocket and I was sliding back the safety with my thumb. I pushed the release. The blade snapped out and I rammed it into Fareed like a punch in the stomach. I felt the initial resistance of the thick wall of his flesh and then the dagger broke through. The blow knocked the wind out of him. As soon as the knife went in I wished I hadn't done it. But it was too late to take it back. His face was inches from mine as he looked at me, wide-eyed with surprise. I could see sweat on his forehead and smell his bitter breath. *It was wrong what you did, but I'm still sorry, man.*

The little room rang with the noise of screaming voices. Pain raced through my jaw as Mahmoud's fist landed there. I pulled the knife from Fareed's belly and turned it around in my hand as I thrust it backward. Horror rolled over the faces of Adir and Tammy. There was a sickening pop and I saw that the blade had gone straight into Mahmoud's eye, right up to the bone handle. He cried out and I could feel his body shaking. Angry and desperate voices were yelling and screaming and there was something warm and wet on my leg. Fareed sank to his knees, holding the wound with both his hands. Mahmoud staggered and fell back onto the bench. With the bloody knife in my hand I turned to face Adir, who continued choking Tammy in his elbow. She was gasping and her face was swollen and red. Nigel was still frozen on the bench.

Adir looked terrified. In the brightness of the bare bulb I could see sweat running down his face. The sound of his panting filled the room.

"C'mon, man," I said. "I don't want to hurt you. Please just let her go."

From the corner of my eye I saw Marissa lunge to grab something on the floor near Mahmoud. In the next instant it looked as though she were pounding her fist onto Adir's foot. He yelled in pain and I saw blood ooze up through his shoe. And then I realized she was holding Mahmoud's pocket-knife. In a split second Tammy pulled away from Adir and I threw myself at him, driving the switchblade between his ribs and then yanking it out fast. He slammed his fist into my kidney before I could jump back. Adir moved his hands over the gash and looked at me in horror, just as I leapt at him again. He fell to the floor on his back, staring shocked at the ceiling and holding his neck as blood foamed between his fingers. My heart was pounding. I knelt down and grabbed his shoulder and belt and flipped him over, face-down on the concrete floor. A few feet away Mahmoud lay motionless on the bench, blood streaking down from his eye. Fareed was kneeling on the floor holding his stomach. His face was waxy and pale.

"Nigel, smother him with a cushion," Marissa said. "Hurry, man, do it fast!"

"Fuck that," he croaked. "No way."

"For God's sake, I'll do it, then!"

She stepped from the doorway over Adir's body.

"No, Marissa, don't!" Tammy yelled, reaching out as if to stop her but then pulling back.

Marissa put her foot on Fareed's shoulder and pushed him to the floor. His head hit the cement. She grabbed a red cushion from the bench and with both hands pressed it over his face.

"What was that you said about it being very bad for the women? HUH, MOTHERFUCKER?!"

She raised her body on her arms to bring all of her weight onto the cushion. I felt sorry for him but it was too late now. He weakly tried to push her away and then his body became still.

"I think the son of a bitch is dead," Marissa said, standing up and looking at me wild-eyed. Her face was slick with sweat.

"Oh, sweet Lord Jesus!" Tammy sobbed.

Nigel jumped over the bodies and took Tammy's hand, pulling her out of the room. I heard him throwing up.

Blood was spreading on the floor around Adir as he lay face-down and motionless. Tammy and Nigel were huddled in the darkness of the raw space, crying with their arms around each other. The air smelled of vomit and fish and the only light came from inside the room with the bodies, a dim column across the dusty floor.

Before it happened, if I had imagined being in a situation like this one I would have expected to feel scared and sick. But I didn't feel that way. Maybe some self-preserving instinct had awakened within me, but I experienced an odd sense of equanimity and power.

"We've got to get out of here right now!" Nigel said, his voice cracking.

"No. Not yet. We have to think this through."

"Will is right," Marissa said. "Everybody cool it!"

"Oh, my God, Clark," Tammy moaned. "What have you gotten us into?"

"Are you insane?" Marissa hissed at Tammy. "He just saved your life! And it was your idea to follow those assholes off the train in the first place!"

"You can go to hell," Tammy said. "I saw what you did in there. I would rather have given them the thousand dollars, and then thrown away that goddamned hashish!" She started sobbing again.

"That would not have been the end of it," I said, hearing the flat, detached sound of my own voice. "The police would have shown up five minutes later."

"We should go to the police now," Nigel said. "We have to tell them everything!"

"And spend the rest of our lives in some third-world dungeon? No way. These guys work together with the police."

"It was self-defense, man!"

"I didn't see you defending anyone, Nigel," Marissa said.

"Or killing anyone, either!" Tammy yelled at her.

"Keep your voices down," I whispered. "The old couple must still be asleep, and that's the way we want it."

"Oh, my God," Tammy said, "them!"

"The cops are gonna come through this door at any minute," Nigel said, shaking with fear. "Let's get the fuck out of here and go back to Spain!"

"Listen to me," I said. "I read the schedule when we got off the train. The last one for Rabat leaves here at twelve-thirty, which is in forty minutes. We have to be on that train. We'll get there at dawn."

"You want us to go farther into the country?" Tammy

said, wiping tears and mucus onto her sleeve. "Are you nuts? We have to go back to Spain!"

"How, through Tangier? There's no train north until seven o'clock tomorrow morning. We can't stay here that long. From Rabat we can get a plane or a boat back to Europe. There's no record of us ever being here, only that we got off the ferry in Tangier and then boarded the train to Rabat."

"He's right," Marissa said. "It'll be like we were never here."

Tammy stopped crying and glared at her friend. "Are you crazy? With all the witnesses who saw us with these guys? The man at the restaurant, and the one at the carpet shop?"

"They don't know our names," Marissa said. "And we all look alike to them."

"This is terrible!" Nigel groaned. Tears were sliding down his face.

I looked back into the room where the bodies were lying on the floor and bench. "We have to make it appear that a drug deal went bad between these three." I stepped over Adir's blood and with a sock from Nigel's backpack picked Mahmoud's pocketknife up off the floor. I crouched by Fareed's body and lifted the cushion off his face. His eyes stared lifelessly at the ceiling. His mouth was open and there were purple blotches on his face and lips. I pushed the blade of the pocketknife into the wound in his belly and left it there.

"Make sure the hash is in plain sight."

Marissa set the kilo on the bench.

"My God, Will, you're covered in blood."

I looked down at myself—sticky red caked my jeans, shirt and hands. Tammy and Nigel were pacing in the dim unfinished space. "Get your bags out of the room," I told them. "And check to see if you have blood on your clothes. We'll have to stuff them into one of the cement bags. Make sure you empty your pockets first."

Marissa stood watching me as I stripped down to my socks and briefs. One side of her glowed in the low light from the room; the other half was lost in shadow. She unbuckled her black leather belt and unzipped her jeans, wriggling as she pushed them down over her hips, past her knees and calves and over her bare feet. She stared at me with intense eyes as she lifted the blood-stained tank top over her head. She was wearing a black bra and panties and her bare skin was shiny and taut in the shadowy light. She glanced down at my crotch and then up at my eyes.

Carrying the clothes I crossed the floor to where the bags of cement mix lay propped against the far wall in the darkness. One of the bags was half-empty and I bent down and unfolded the stiff brown paper, reaching inside and feeling the hard mixture on the bottom. I checked the pockets of both pairs of jeans and then shoved them into the bag with the T-shirts.

Tammy and Nigel had removed their bags from the room with the bodies and were changing in the pale light outside the door of the second bedroom. She was crying again. From where I knelt Tammy was a towering silhouette as she crossed the space to hand me the bloodied clothes, her shadow falling over me.

"We're going to be okay," I said, gently squeezing her bare leg. She pulled away.

There wasn't much room left in the cement bag. I leaned onto Tammy and Nigel's clothes with both hands, trying to compress them. The middle of the bag started to rip. When I entered the bedroom Marissa was dressed in her black leggings and a long denim shirt that hung down like a skirt.

"We need something to tie this up."

"I've got a clothesline in my backpack," she said.

"Perfect, get it."

"What are you gonna do with the cement bag?"

"Throw it over the seawall."

My hands were covered with dried blood and gray dust. I searched my duffel bag and found some packets of moistened napkins. I threw a couple at her feet. "Clean yourself up and then put the towelettes inside the cement bag with the clothes." I put on a clean shirt and khakis and started making the bed. "We were never here. Make sure you don't leave anything in this room."

Marissa found the clothesline. Tammy appeared in the doorway. "Take some of these and clean your hands and face," I said.

Tammy didn't look at me. "We already cleaned up. We're ready to go."

"Where'd you put the dirty napkins?"

"I don't know, I think Nigel stuck them in his backpack."

"Well, take them out of there. We're gonna put everything in this cement bag and then throw it into the Atlantic. Wipe off your shoes, too."

With the duffel and my canvas satchel over my shoulder I used both hands to hoist the cement bag against my chest. Passing the other room I saw Adir's legs across the floor. Old smoke and the stink of death rotted the air.

At the door to the stairs I put a pair of my underwear over the knob and tried to turn it. "We're locked in here."

"Oh, Christ!" Tammy said.

I pressed my ear against the door but heard nothing.

"We'll have to go out through the roof. Try to cover over those shoeprints in the dust."

The steps to the roof were made of two-by-fours. I bent my head down and went up through the opening in the ceiling. Outside on the flat roof I could feel the ocean breeze. Stars burned across the moonless sky. For an instant I let myself feel relief.

Tammy knelt by the parapet. "It must be twenty feet down."

I looked at the rooftops of the other houses, next door and across the chasm of the alley, all the same height, with clothes moving on lines. On my wristwatch I saw the time glowing in the dark: twelve-fifteen. The train would leave in fifteen minutes. I could barely make out the ground below. The street seemed empty but I knew men might be lurking in the doorways.

"We'll drop the bags to cushion our fall," I said. "And then Nigel can jump first. I'll lower you and Marissa down so you won't have as far to fall. Then I'll drop the cement bag and go down last. Just make sure you get out of the way."

"What if someone sees us?" Nigel said. His legs were shaking.

"The train stops here in fifteen minutes. Get on with it."

I swung my duffel over the edge of the parapet, lowered it as far as I could, and then let go. I heard the nylon scraping the stucco wall; there was a beat of silence and then a thwack as the bag hit the ground.

"Give me the next one."

Marissa handed me her backpack and a smaller shoulder bag. A minute later all of our bags were over the side.

"All right, Nigel. You're up."

He looked at me with pallid trepidation, rubbing his palms on his hips.

"It's okay, honey," Tammy told him. "You'll be all right."

Crouching, Nigel grasped the inside edge of the parapet and gingerly moved his knees over the side. Suddenly his torso dropped out of sight; his fingers held for a second and then slipped off the side. There was a tumbling thud and we heard Nigel groan in pain.

Tammy nimbly swung her long legs over, holding to the top for a moment and then dropping into the darkness. Her landing barely made a sound.

Marissa threw her arms around my neck and kissed me

on the mouth. "Hold my hand," she said, climbing over the edge. She was looking at me as she pushed away from the wall. I heard a soft thump. I lifted the heavy cement bag over the parapet and let it drop. It landed with a loud smacking sound that echoed down the alley.

I jumped. My feet hit the duffel and I rolled onto the other bags, scraping my palm against the street.

Nigel was bending down and rubbing his ankle. "Shite, I think I broke it," he said, hissing between his teeth.

I picked up my duffel and satchel and the cement bag and headed around the corner toward the seawall. Ahead of us the alley disappeared in darkness. I didn't see anyone. The path ended and we turned to the right. The booming of the waves on the rocks was much louder here and I felt the muscles in my legs tighten as the street began to incline.

Light fell from an open doorway. I glanced inside as we passed; a man was sitting on an overturned bucket, surrounded by red fishing nets on the floor. Arabic music played on a distorted radio.

We came upon an overlook from the seawall. The noise of the waves grew still louder and the air was misty with sea spray. There were waist-high notches along the top of the parapet. I set the cement bag in one of them. The bottom and sides were ripped from the fall but the bag still held together.

"Does the water come right up to the wall?" Marissa asked.

All I could see were stars over the ocean. "I'm not sure."

"If you drop the bag straight down, it might land on the rocks. People will be able to spot it!"

"Maybe we should take it down to the beach," Tammy said.

"There's no time for that."

I reached into my pocket for the switchblade. The handle was sticky with drying blood. Leaning through a notch in the parapet I turned my head to one side and tried to listen to the water. It sounded like the waves were breaking about twenty feet out and then rinsing through the spaces between the rocks. I took a step back and then sprung my body forward, throwing the knife with all my strength. It spun end-over-end in a high arc and quickly disappeared into the darkness. All I could hear were the waves.

"Nigel, grab one end."

Facing one another we began swinging the cement bag in a pendulum motion.

"One ..."

We swung the bag back and forth.

"Two ... three!"

We stumbled against the parapet as the bag became airborne over the side and then instantly sank out of sight. Three heartbeats later I heard it smash on the rocks. The sound vanished under the booming surf.

Even as she stood a few feet in front of me, Tammy's face was lost in darkness. I picked up my bags and continued walking along the top of the seawall toward the square. The pathway declined and we came to the base of the high thick wall around the medina. The space between the rampart and the houses was only a few feet wide here, and pitch black. At first I had to feel my way along the rough wall.

I heard Nigel grunt in pain, followed by the sound of his bag hitting the ground. "Shite, my ankle!"

I started walking faster. Marissa's steps quickened behind me.

We reached the big rounded gate in the wall. I paused for a second to let Marissa come beside me. *"We're tourists having fun,"* I whispered. Holding hands and smiling we emerged into the dark plaza. I became aware of the figures of several men sitting on the ground with their backs against the rampart wall. They said nothing as we walked across the square toward the faint light of the train station, a shack and canopy alongside the tracks. The sea was quieter here and our shoes crunched on the pebbles. And then from a distance behind us rose the sound of rough voices and Nigel's Irish brogue.

Just then Marissa said: *"Here comes the train."*

Through the darkness I could see its headlight growing larger by the second. Marissa and I were about ten yards from the station.

"Stay here."

I dropped my bags and ran back across the plaza. In the moonless night I could barely discern the shapes of Tammy and Nigel standing amongst the men. Drawing closer I heard her voice and saw that one of them was gripping her arm while Nigel pleaded with him to let her go.

The figure holding Tammy turned to face me. His eyes were concealed in shadow but I recognized him as one of the young men we had seen on the corner earlier that night, the one with the purple mark on his cheek. I swung my arm and my fist slammed into his jaw with a cracking sound, sending a bolt of pain through my wrist and forearm. He staggered and fell back, pulling Tammy down with him. I could hear the train clanging and whistling as it reached the station. Three other men advanced on us. I kicked the one with the birthmark hard in the ribs, knocking him back across the pebbles and pulling Tammy from his grip. I seized her bag with one hand and her elbow with the other, lifting her to her feet as we began a dash across the plaza toward the station. Nigel followed, grunting in pain. My mouth was dry and my temples were pounding and air heaved through my windpipe. I let go of Tammy's arm and grabbed my bags off the ground. We reached the platform and jumped aboard the train with Marissa just before the doors closed.

The train was quiet and dark and I waited until I was sure the others were asleep before I looked in my bag for the photograph. I shone my flashlight on the picture. It was Fareed, all right. As the train rolled on I opened the window further, ripped the picture into pieces and tossed them out into the night.

Chapter Four

A FEW DAYS EARLIER I had been in Madrid, eating lunch in a diner and thinking about the Dutchman's offer. I knew the proposition was horrific. But knowing had never done me much good before. Struggling with the storm in my head I was surprised to see a blonde walking by on the sidewalk. Sunlight reflected off her long hair. She was carrying a backpack and black leggings squeezed her curves. For the first time since I had arrived the sense of freedom and possibility that travel always promises finally began to spark within me. But my dilemma remained.

After lunch I went to the park at the end of the block, where old men were standing around watching each other play chess on stone tables. A mustachioed gentleman in a brown suit and fedora walked with comically upright posture, bellowing "LOTERIA!" and waving a wad of tickets. There was an opera house at one end of the rectangular park, white in the sun, and a hotel with green awnings at the other. Along the sides were restaurants and bars under apartments with boxy lacquered-wood balconies screened with latticework grilles. A slim street angled away from the park—one side warm in sunlight, the other damp in shadow and stinking of stale beer and piss. There were bullfight posters on the buildings, the paper bumpy over the stone walls. I passed a café with open doors where another group of short old men stood drinking coffee at a white marble bar with no stools. The floor was littered with cigarette butts and empty sugar packets.

Farther down there was a cutlery shop where knives glinted in the window. A man in the doorway was smoking a cigarette. I hesitated for a minute and then approached him. He led me to the back of the cluttered little store, past kitchen and hunting knives displayed in glass cases. From under the counter he brought out a tray of switchblades of different lengths and types of handles. I asked to see the nine-inch knife with a bone handle and chrome hardware. I slid down the safety and pushed the round release button; the shining blade appeared with a crisp snap. I retracted it into the handle and then snapped it out again. The man chuckled as he looked at me over the rim of his reading glasses. I paid him for the knife and then left. *"It's just in case,"* I told myself. *"I haven't decided anything yet."*

There was a coffee shop and bakery on the corner. Streets on either side angled to a point at a traffic circle; the shop was wedge-shaped with windows overlooking motorcycles and tiny cars whipping around and shooting off in five directions. The blonde I had seen walking past the diner was sitting inside the café, drinking coffee and reading a newspaper. My heart beat a little faster as I opened the door and went in. The air was warm with coffee and pastries. I ordered tea and sat at a table with a clear view of the girl's face. She had a little nose, creamy cheeks and plump lips. She had removed her jacket; a sleeveless aquamarine top revealed slender arms and golden skin. She looked up from her newspaper and saw me staring at her. I pretended to be gazing out the window but felt my face redden. She stood and set a few coins on the table and then walked out of the shop. As she strode past the window she turned and gave me a petulant glance. I hated to see her go but was glad she had noticed me.

I finished my tea and left the bakery. There were short buildings along the street, peeling yellow paint, with small iron balconies. The pensión where I was staying was on the right. The rooms overlooking the street were all taken and I had been forced to settle for my windowless cell in the building's interior. I reached the entrance and was walking into the dark corridor just as the elevator slammed to a stop on the first floor. The blonde walked out toward me.

"Hi," I blurted. "Did you just arrive in Madrid?"

She stopped, looking at me suspiciously. "Yeah, on the train this morning."

"I'm staying here, too. Not bad for the price. Good location."

Her expression was guarded. "What's around here?"

"Lots of restaurants and clubs, but they don't get going until late. I'm Will Clark, from Chicago."

"Stacey Snow," she said, a little warmer now. "From Grand Rapids, Michigan."

"Isn't that funny? We're both Midwesterners."

A Vespa shot down the street and the noise rang through the corridor.

"You're traveling alone?"

"I'm very independent," she said, looking away from me.

Getting my first close look I could see that she was even more gorgeous than I had realized—a glowing face with brows naturally arched over blue eyes.

"Too independent to hang out with me this afternoon?"

A slight smile curled her lips. "I'm on my way to see Retiro Park, if you'd like to tag along."

It was almost noon and the sun shone through a cloudless sky. My spirits lifted as Stacey and I walked together past restaurants, cafés, slot-machine parlors, drugstores and tobacco shops. We saw a deli where salt-cured hams hung in mesh bags from the ceiling. For the first time in days the torturous thoughts were gone from my mind.

"How long have you been in Madrid?" she asked me.

"Couple of days."

"What have you been doing since you got here?"

"Not much. Mostly walking around. And sleeping."

"Sleeping?" She sputtered through her lips. "I hate sleeping. I only do it when I'm really bored."

"Were you bored enough to sleep last night?"

"Only for a few hours. I think I turned off the light at about three a.m."

We approached a corner near a subway entrance where beggars were sitting on the curb. One man's right arm was missing below the elbow. He waved his abbreviated appendage at the passersby, shaking a paper cup with his other hand. The man grinned at me, revealing broken brown teeth. Next to him a small woman in a coarse skirt sat on the pavement with her legs splayed, staring morosely at the ground. The sight of the beggars broke my idyll but Stacey barely seemed to notice them; she said nothing and looked straight ahead. We passed a few more side streets and then turned onto the avenue Paseo del Prado. The buildings had spires and baroque designs.

At a traffic signal she turned to look at my eyes that were shaded by sunglasses.

"What do you do for a living? You're too old to be a student."

It was a question I always dreaded. "I'm a freelance journalist."

The light changed and we started across the street.

"What kind of stuff do you write?"

"Features for newspapers and magazines, profiles, travel, whatever." I wanted to change the subject. "How about you, still in school?"

"Wait," she said, narrowing her eyes at me. "You're here

to write an article?"

"Yeah, about gorgeous blond American girls traveling alone in Spain. What should I call it?" I smiled, but she seemed annoyed. "I'm meeting some friends here, and then we're heading down to Morocco for a few weeks," I said. "It's supposed to be an amazing country, beautiful and exotic—and cheap. The trip is just for fun, but if I find something good to write about, I might try to sell a couple of pieces." My stomach twisted as I spoke. "What about you, what are you doing in Madrid?"

"Why are you a freelancer?" she persisted. "Why don't you get a regular job?"

"No one's hiring. Not white males, anyway. The last job went to a Hispanic lesbian."

Stacey rolled her eyes. "It figures. But do the newspapers ever send you on trips for free?"

I laughed. "They're way too cheap for that."

"Do the articles pay well?"

"Not even close."

Her expression was incredulous. "Then why do you do it? How can you?"

"I like the freedom, I guess. And I'm hoping it will lead to something better, but so far it's just led to more of the same. This time I managed to arrange a free flight from one of the tourism boards, though."

She smirked. "I've been in Europe for two months now. I'm seeing how much of my father's money I can spend."

I didn't say anything. I was fifteen when my dad was shot. His wound became infected and he died five weeks later.

Stacey seemed to notice that my mood had changed. "Have you been to Madrid before?" she asked in a brighter tone.

"Two years ago, right after Clinton won the ninety-two election. I was in Barcelona when the results were announced. In the hotel room you had to put coins in the TV to make it run. And then I came here on the train."

"Clinton?" she said. "Don't get me started. I'm a hardcore Republican."

As we reached a corner the light turned red but she kept going. Cars were rushing toward us and I stepped faster to catch up with her. We crossed the street and walked along in silence for a few minutes and then stopped to buy a couple of Cokes at a newsstand. Sex magazines were on prominent display but Stacey either didn't notice them or pretended not to.

At Retiro Park we walked along the paths and sat under a tree by the pond. On the other side of the water there was a monument with a white colonnade that curved behind a black statue of a man on horseback. White steps led down to the water. A few people were relaxing there in the sun. It felt good to sit in the shade, cross-legged on the grass. The air was fragrant from the flowers planted alongside the path. A breeze moved the leaves in the trees and shadows played across the lawn.

"I have to admit," I said, "I'm a little surprised that you're traveling alone. Don't you have a boyfriend?"

"You're a nosy bastard, aren't you?"

"And you're a real charmer."

Stacey sipped her soda and looked at the people rowing small boats on the water. I took off my sunglasses and squinted as I looked at her. She seemed startled by my eyes.

"When did you say you're leaving?"

"In two more days," I said. "This girl Marissa is supposed to arrive here from Paris tomorrow, and then the next night we're meeting our other friends and taking the train south to Algeciras."

"Marissa is your girlfriend?"

I chuckled. "No, I can't stand her, to tell you the truth. She's friends with my friend Tammy. More like one of Tammy's sycophants, actually."

"You and Tammy are just friends?"

"Yeah. We were classmates in college."

A gypsy woman approached us, holding out her hand. She wore a tattered headscarf and was carrying a sleeping infant in a sling on her back. "Please," the Roma moaned, "my baby needs milk."

I looked around to see if anyone else had crept up on us. "No, I'm sorry," I told her. She was still standing there with her hand out, grimacing.

"He said, 'No!'" Stacey yelled. The gypsy dropped her hand and walked away, muttering. "Goddamn beggars," Stacey said. "They shouldn't have kids."

I didn't like her attitude, but my God, she was a knockout. She had a perfect shape, with skin to match. I wanted to kiss her skin.

"How long will you be here?" I said.

"Only until tomorrow morning. Then I'm going to Seville."

I tried not to show my disappointment. "You just got here this morning, and you're already leaving tomorrow?"

"I'm restless," she said, looking away from me. "I usually don't stay in any city for more than one night."

"How much longer are you planning to travel?"

"I don't know. Until I get bored."

We sat there in silence for a few minutes, looking at the reflection of the white pillars across the surface of the pond. Finally she asked: "Where are you going in Morocco, Will?"

"At Algeciras we'll take the ferry to Tangier. From there, trains down to Rabat and then to Marrakesh. And then maybe a bus over the mountains, into the desert." A sick feeling crawled through my guts.

"I was thinking about going to Morocco after Seville."

"You might as well," I said, trying to play it cool. "It's so close, and yet it's like stepping back in time, into another world. That's what I've heard, anyway."

"I was thinking the same thing, that I might as well go and see it," she said.

"It can be a little dangerous down there, too. You have to be careful. The hustlers will pounce all over you."

The petulant look that I had seen several times since meeting her now reappeared on Stacey's face. But her aloofness and irascibility only increased my attraction to her.

"I can take care of myself," she said.

"Maybe we can meet up along the way. I should be in Rabat in a few days, at the Hotel Splendide."

"My only plan is to leave for Seville tomorrow morning."

A black squirrel dashed past us on the grass. Stacey paid no attention to the little animal. Sunlight dropped through the trees, casting dappled shadows across her face. A group of teenagers was suddenly clamoring on the path behind us, blasting dance music from a boom box.

"What are you doing tonight?" I asked her. "Wanna have dinner with me?"

Stacey gave me an appraising look, but then her expression softened. "All right," she said. "I guess I could use the company."

We agreed to meet in front of the hostel at eight-thirty, and then Stacey said she had to go. My heart bounced as I watched her walk away, shapely in black stretch fabric.

Chapter Five

I DIDN'T REALLY EXPECT Stacey to keep our date, so I was surprised and happy to find her waiting for me in front of the pensión, wearing a little black dress and high-heeled sandals. Her toenails were painted and the straps of her shoes wrapped around her ankles. Her breasts were medium-sized and beautifully shaped, her cleavage achingly lovely. She smiled when she saw me and I kissed her on the cheek. She smelled like perfume, a sexy nighttime scent. We walked together to the nightlife district near the hostel and drank a few sangrias in a bar before strolling to a corner restaurant where we sat by a window and could see people moving through the darkness and bright color outside. She ordered fried fish that came to the table whole, with the eye staring up; I had grilled steak served with roasted vegetables and potatoes. We continued drinking sangria during dinner and were both a bit drunk.

"How old are you?" she said, looking at me dubiously.

"Twenty-nine. How old are you?"

"Twenty-three." She paused, looked at the table and then said: "Will, you're not worried about your future?"

"In what sense?"

"Your career. You're too smart to waste your life as an underpaid freelance reporter. Don't you want to make some money, for God's sake?"

The words rattled around inside me. I wouldn't dare tell her that I owed more on my student loans and credit cards than I had made during the previous year. In my mind's eye I saw the stranger's face pass from the darkness of the alley into the brief light of the streetlamp, and the clean-cut Dutchman walking beside me along the canals.

"I'll make some money eventually," I said, reaching under the table to squeeze Stacey's bare leg.

She slapped away my hand. "Don't you think about your future?"

"Not really," I lied. "What about you, what's in your future?"

Someone dropped a plate in the back of the restaurant. "I have a marketing degree from the University of Michigan. I'll be just fine." She took another long drink from her glass of wine. Stacey looked at me with boozy blue eyes and smiled with straight white teeth that made her seem expensive and luxurious, intensely desirable, out of my league. Her lips looked plump and kissable and her cheeks were red from the sangria.

After dinner we stumbled through alleys paved with bricks and smeared with neon color. Twenty-year-olds stood on the corners or ambled past the sidewalk cafés, laughing and shouting to one another. Occasionally a small car would crawl by with only a couple feet of space on either side.

Stacey caught me looking down her cleavage and gave me a sexy eye. As we turned a corner I wrapped my arm around her shoulders—she laughed and began to collapse against me, but then pulled away. "Jess watch it, buster," she slurred.

She was smiling and capering down the alley when we found the open door of a nightclub. A rock band was playing on a tiny stage inside.

"Wanna go in?"

A devilish smoke seemed to drift across her eyes as the lids became heavier and the corners of her mouth curled up. "No," she said, still looking at the band. "Let's go back to the pensión."

She took my hand and we began walking fast. We turned a dark corner and I pulled her against me, kissing her mouth and holding her around the waist, pressing our pelvises together. She was deliriously soft and warm and perfumed and her dress was a wisp against her body. She slipped her arms around my neck. As we kissed I could feel waves of heat rising from my groin and spreading through my chest and arms. My heart was pounding. I dropped my right hand to her derrière, squeezing the firm curve as our tongues twirled together. I felt myself hardening against her, and I knew that she could feel it, too.

"C'mon," she said in a husky voice. "Let's go back to my room."

As we hurried up the block I noticed people looking at us, as if our intentions were clear to see. We crossed Calle Principe to the pensión. The heavy wooden doors were locked.

"Shit, we'll have to buzz the old man who runs the place," Stacey said. "But he can't know we're coming in together."

I wondered if she was losing her nerve. "I don't think he would care. But you can go up first, and I'll be there ten minutes later. What's your room number?"

"It's the first door on the right."

"You got a room in front, with a balcony?"

"Yeah, why?"

"Never mind. I'll meet you up there in ten minutes."

"I'll leave my door unlocked." She pulled me toward her and kissed me, and then turned to ring the buzzer, shooing me away with her other hand.

At the end of the block I turned onto a dark street. Empty storefronts painted black. It was quiet and there was no one around. I didn't notice the kids sitting in a doorway until I heard the girl's voice: "*Haa-sheeeesh*...." I stopped but couldn't see her face in the shadows.

"You want some hashish? Good stuff, from Morocco."

"Let's see it," I said, looking down the street behind me. "C'mon, quick."

"Relax, American," the girl said. "The *policia* turn a blind eye."

Before she could hand me the hash a group of Spaniards rounded the corner, men and women shouting and laughing. I walked away and at the end of the block turned back toward the hostel.

Señor Augusto buzzed me in and a minute later the little elevator was shaking up past the darkened floors. When it reached four I could see him standing in the doorway wearing a bathrobe, wiry white hair sticking out from the sides of his bald head.

"Buenas noches, Señor Clark," he said, stepping aside to let me pass. Behind him the pensión was silent and dark except for an orange glow around the lamp in the sitting room.

He handed me my room key. "A girl called for you," he said, a little louder.

I glanced toward Stacey's room. "What did she say?" I whispered.

"She'll get here tomorrow afternoon at four. I reserved room number three for her." He turned to lock the door.

"Gracias, señor. Hasta mañana."

I passed through the sitting area and felt my way down the murky corridor, stopping at my room and turning the key in the lock. It snapped through the silence. Inside the room I closed the door and flicked on the light and then waited for the old man to walk past on his way back to his family's apartment on the other side of the wall at the end of the hall.

I heard his slippers padding past. I waited for the sound of the door to his apartment closing, and then to be sure I waited a couple of minutes more. After removing my jacket and shoes I cracked open the door. The hallway was dim toward the sitting room, black in the other direction. I stepped softly down the corridor and through the sitting room. There was an alcove in the wall with doors facing each other on either side. I placed my hand on the knob to the right and tightened my fingers around it. For a minute I didn't move. Then I eased open the door.

Inside the room there were no lights and at first I couldn't see anything. And then I turned and saw that Stacey had opened the French doors to the little balcony and was standing naked in silhouette against the light from the street. I could see the graceful curves of her hips and breasts in sharp outline, the firm muscles of her thighs and a fluff of light hair between her legs. Her arms and shoulders were thin and delicate and her long hair spilled over her skin.

Wet heat rose undulating through my body. I pulled off my socks and jeans and unbuttoned my shirt and dropped it on the floor. In my briefs I crossed the room to Stacey, wrapping one arm around her neck and the other around her waist. *"My darling girl."* She pushed my underwear down over my hips.

I WAS STARTING TO FALL ASLEEP when she shoved my shoulder.

"You have to go back to your room. You can't sleep in here."

My head was filled with cement from the wine. "What's the big deal?"

She got out of the bed and started picking my clothes off the floor and throwing them at me. "C'mon. You have to go!"

The narrow bed squeaked as I swung my legs over the side. I stood and my head thudded inside as I turned to look at Stacey. She was putting on pajamas.

"I need to get some sleep," she said.

"Am I boring you?"

Her expression softened. "I would rather have you stay, but I don't want the old man to see you leaving my room in the morning."

"All right," I said, reluctantly dressing myself. "But let's have breakfast together before you go."

"Sure. Meet me downstairs at nine-thirty."

I hugged her. "I'll see you then."

Stacey seemed distant now, avoiding my eyes. "Okay," she said. "Good night."

Chapter Six

MY SLEEP WAS ROILED with violent dreams. From my angle of lying on the ground looking up at him I saw the stranger's face pass from the darkness into the light of the streetlamp. I felt the punch in my stomach and the kick in my side and I heard them laughing as they ran away. Several times during the night I woke with a dry thirst and took long gulps of tepid water from a bottle on the table by the bed.

I had set my alarm for nine and was afraid of missing Stacey, so I hurried to shower and dress. On my way out I saw the door to her room was open. The room was bright in the morning sunlight and the bed was already made. I stuck my head inside and saw that her backpack was gone. Señor Augusto's wife was sweeping the floor.

"Good morning, señora. Did Señorita Snow leave already?"

The old woman looked at me with a sympathetic face. "Yes, early this morning."

"Well, then she must be on her way to Seville by now," I said, handing the señora my key and trying to seem undisturbed by the news. "Gracias."

As the elevator rattled down past the dark floors I felt my mood sink along with it. Outside I looked at the wall by the spot where we had first spoken the morning before, standing there for a few minutes and looking up and down the block. The sunlight seared my eyes and a dull pain tightened my forehead and the back of my neck.

For the next few hours I walked in aimless loops through the city, thinking about Stacey, the stranger and the Dutchman's offer. A couple of times on the street I thought I saw the gaze of a passerby linger too long on me. I reached into my pocket and squeezed the handle of the knife.

In the late afternoon I returned to the pensión and fell asleep. I was dreaming about my studio apartment in Chicago when a loud knock on the door jolted me awake. It was the señora.

I pulled on my jeans and opened the door. "What is it?"

"Señorita Wright has arrived." The old woman pointed down the hall toward the sitting room.

Marissa was the last person I wanted to see. "Okay, señora, I'll be right there. Thank you."

I closed the door and bent to see my reflection in the small mirror on the wall. My dirty blond hair was sticking out on one side. I tried to smooth it down but couldn't salve the discomfort I felt in my own skin, the mocking dissatisfaction I had always harbored for myself. But there was no time to think about that now.

At the end of the unlit hall Marissa was standing in the pink glow of the sitting room, looking at me not happily, but expectantly. She was tomboyish with her short spiky dark hair, black tights and green army jacket. Her face was pretty but tough looking. She was only twenty-six but incessant scowling had already carved a vertical furrow in the skin of her forehead just above the space between her eyes. I smiled and extended my hand to her.

"How's it goin'?"

She accepted my hand but quickly released it, an impatient expression on her face.

"Good, Will. What were you doing, sleeping?"

"Yeah, for a little bit. How was your trip?"

Marissa slid her backpack off her shoulders and onto the floor, smiling as mischief played across her eyes. "The train from Paris was *awesome*. Have you heard from Tammy and Nigel?"

"No, but we're supposed to meet them at the train station tomorrow night at ten. Are you hungry?"

"Starved."

"Why don't you put your things away and we'll go get some tapas before the bars close for the afternoon. After that we won't be able to eat until nine o'clock."

"Okay, just let me take a quick shower first."

Marissa bent down to unzip her backpack and pulled out a book. From between the pages she removed a couple of photocopies. "A guy on the train gave me this essay about human rights. You *have* to read it. It'll only take you a few minutes."

I wasn't in the mood, but tried to be polite. "Okay, cool. I'll check it out."

On the loveseat in the sitting room I read the first couple of sentences, something about militias butchering people in Algeria. But my mind soon wandered. I was thinking about Stacey.

Suddenly Marissa was standing in front of me, showered and ready. "What'd 'ja think? Unbelievable, huh?"

"Um, I haven't finished it yet...."

"What? The whole thing's only two pages long!"

"I'll finish it later."

Marissa rolled her eyes. "Whatever. Let's go."

We left the hostel and walked toward the traffic circle. It was about five o'clock but the sun was still high and the day felt young. Darkness wouldn't drop until after nine. We turned through a pedestrian area filled with café tables that would be empty until the dinner crowds arrived hours later. I led Marissa around the corner to a tapas bar. We opened the door into a tiny space with a wood counter and a few stools. Yellowing lacquered newspaper pages covered the walls. The man behind the bar handed us a menu. Behind him on a countertop a salt-cured pig's leg was held horizontally in a vice. The man ran a blade along its length, peeling off long thin slices of prosciutto, which he piled onto a plate with bread and set before us.

"Mmm, this is really good," Marissa said, narrowing her eyes as she chewed.

I was surprised that she even ate meat. I ordered for both of us: a bottle of sherry, a plate of olives and a Spanish omelet.

"Tell me about Paris."

A smug expression crossed Marissa's face and she shifted in her seat. "I met a jazz musician." She looked at me and grinned, stretching a long piece of ham away from her teeth.

"Yeah, in Paris?"

"He was this *beautiful* black man, Alain. He plays saxophone in a little club near Les Halles. We had a *wild* night together." Marissa crossed her legs and sipped the sherry. She popped an olive into her mouth and chewed it sensuously.

I sipped the dry white wine, enjoying the slight burn as it spread down my throat and through my chest. I knew she was trying to goad me. I took a bite of the omelet and looked at her, reminded of the conflicting attraction and dislike that she had always aroused within me. We had a history of even the most seemingly innocent conversations quickly degrading into arguments and misunderstandings. When she saw that I wasn't going to take the bait about the jazz musician she changed the subject and started talking superciliously about "postmodernism." What a pain in the ass, I thought. I wished I were with Stacey instead of this insufferable girl.

Marissa would ruin everything. She turned and pretended to be reading the headlines on the walls, but I knew she didn't understand Spanish. On the opposite wall a big shiny red cockroach crawled up the buckled newsprint.

THAT NIGHT WE ATE PIZZA for dinner and walked around in the nightlife district. With Stacey gone and Marissa here my mood was sour and I told myself that I would accept the Dutchman's proposition. In that dark gravity it seemed I had no other prospects. I led Marissa into the alley where I had seen the girl selling hashish the night before. She looked disapprovingly into the darkness but didn't argue. The street was lost in shadow and at first it was difficult to see anything. I squinted into the gloom, looking for the girl. But the doorways were empty. We continued up the block, seeing no one. At the corner we turned onto the main drag, a jolting contrast of noisy bright electric color, people at café tables drinking and laughing, the smoky smell of meat and seafood grilling.

The main street ended in a T-shape at the last alley, where there was a bar with a red-and-yellow neon sign: "*Caliente*." A sexy woman with long black hair was standing in the street with two men, wearing an outfit that showed lots of tanned skin. She gave me a teasing glance as we passed. The sight of her made me miss Stacey. Farther down the block I stopped in front of a club that had no sign and only a green fluorescent light over the door.

"Let's check this place out."

Marissa seemed apprehensive as she looked through the windows into the dark club, but then she said: "Fine. Let's go."

I opened the door and we walked into the spicy-chocolate aroma of hashish smoke. In the low greenish light young men sat at a dozen small tables, rolling and smoking cigarettes. Music on the stereo was a fusion of North African melodies and electronic dance beats. Occasional voices we heard were in Arabic.

There was an open table by the far wall. We squeezed through the narrow spaces between the tables, past the backs of the others.

Marissa sat down and I went to the bar. When I returned we drank our beers in silence, looking around the room more than at one another. It appeared that she was the only woman, and we were the only non-Arabs, in the place.

I saw her peering over my shoulder. "The guy behind you is staring at us."

I turned as if to see out the windows, and then glanced at the young man sitting alone. He had dark hair and olive skin and was wearing a black leather jacket and smoking a hand-rolled cigarette. He seemed to be looking at me but it was difficult to discern his dark eyes through the smoke of the dimly lit club. I turned around to face him. "Como esta, señor?"

Without hesitating he pulled his chair over to our table. "You are Americans?" He handed me his burning cigarette.

I brought it close to my mouth without touching the wet paper to my lips, and drew in the heavy smoke. The flavor was a mixture of hashish and tobacco.

"Thank you, señor. Yes, we're from the States."

I exhaled and smoke rolled across the table as I handed the cigarette to Marissa. She took a long drag but said nothing to the man, who gave her an icy look.

"You're from Madrid?" I asked him.

"No. From Morocco."

"Oh yeah? We're going there in a couple of days. I hear it's a very beautiful country."

The man took the *kif* joint from Marissa and hit on it. "Morocco is a poor country," he said, waving his arm. "Life is very difficult there. No jobs. At least in Spain, a man can eat."

He handed the joint back to me and I nodded to him as I inhaled the smoke again. I could already feel the hashish taking effect, hitting me hard on top of the beer. Suddenly the groove of the music moved me as if I were hearing it for the first time. The weak green light, which before had seemed vaguely menacing, became a sensuous refuge.

The man looked at me intently. "You and your wife are here on holiday?"

"On holiday, yes." I looked at Marissa as I handed her the burning joint.

"Is this stuff legal here?" she said, and then drew more smoke into her lungs. I could see she was getting stoned already.

He looked at her with an expression of lust and contempt. "You can possess hashish and smoke it, but you cannot sell it or buy it," he laughed.

"Can I buy you a drink, my friend?" I asked him. "What would you like?"

"A beer. Merci, monsieur."

I stood to walk to the bar, knowing that I was leaving Marissa alone with the stranger just as a soaring hashish buzz was taking flight in her brain. *"I thought you weren't supposed to drink alcohol?"* I heard her saying as I walked away into the green light and loud thumping music. When I returned she was arguing with him.

"In Morocco, the woman keeps her mouth shut," he said to her bitterly.

The scowl that I had seen before was now in full display across Marissa's face. "Well, maybe it's time you moved out of the Stone Age, and into the twentieth century!"

"Hey, hey, *tranquilo, tranquilo,*" I murmured, handing each of them a cold bottle of beer. "Let's be nice and have a drink. C'mon. Salud."

"*Merci,*" the man said, nodding and taking a long sip.

Marissa's face and eyes were red. "He was just telling me that a Moroccan woman would never *dare* show her face in a place like this."

I gave her a hard look. "Different cultures have their own customs," I said, not really believing my own words. "It's not for us to judge."

"Fuck that! I don't respect any custom that degrades women."

"In my father's house the women do not even eat at the same table with the men," the stranger said. "They serve us and then stay in the kitchen, where they belong. If I ever found my woman in a place like this, I would beat her."

Marissa turned and looked at me. "Should we get going?"

I ignored her. "Listen, my friend, I'll give you cab fare home if you let me keep a little smoke for later."

He laughed. "I live far away. A taxi from here will cost me two thousand pesetas."

I knew I had a two-thousand-peseta bill in my pocket. I found the note and set it on the table in front of him. He took the money and removed a plastic bag from an inside pocket of his jacket. It was filled with little rectangles of aluminum foil, one of which he placed on the table. He looked at Marissa; she was turning away from him. The stranger reached into his pocket again and then set an envelope next to the shiny aluminum packet. I slid my hand across the table and took the envelope, quickly putting it inside my jacket. Smoke swirled around us in the airless café. The music was fast and repetitive, hypnotic halftones over a bumping beat. I peeled back the aluminum foil, slicing my thumbnail into the moist clump of hashish. Bringing the gram close to my nose I could smell its thick, resinous aroma. I folded the foil back and put it into my pocket.

"It's been nice to meet you, monsieur. I hope you'll be comfortable in the taxi ride home."

Marissa bolted up and began working her way between the tables toward the exit.

The man looked at me with bloodshot eyes and grinned. "You should teach that wife of yours some manners."

I smiled at him. "She's not my wife, thank God." As I began squeezing through the tight spaces a wave of dizziness tilted my body to one side. Shadowy faces looked up at me with cold expressions. I stumbled into the back of a man's chair and he turned and sneered. "*Pardon, monsieur.*" In the smoky green darkness I couldn't see Marissa; she must have already gone out the door, the location of which I had momentarily misplaced. It swung open as someone entered the café, and I turned and walked out to the street. Marissa was standing there waiting, looking at me with her standard expression of annoyance.

Chapter Seven

WHEN I AWOKE the next morning my head was thumping. As I lay in the bed my thoughts drifted back to Stacey: I remembered our afternoon in the park and the night in her room. I jerked off. Afterwards I still thought of her, but without the sexual desire, and I felt a weary sense of loss. I doubted I would see her again.

After a shower and shave I dressed and headed downstairs to the diner for breakfast. On my way out I looked for Marissa and was relieved to learn from the señora that she had already left for the day to see the sights in Madrid.

I killed a few hours wandering around the city, occasionally stopping to jot notes for a possible article, never with any specific angle in mind. I still had not made a decision. Like shadows across a bright wall my thoughts alternated between dark and light. I doubted I would do it. But then I would get angry again and start thinking about how it might be done.

That afternoon I walked back to the park. On the wide paths vendors were selling handicrafts from carts and I bought a little pipe with a gargoyle face carved around the bowl. I was anxious about meeting Tammy and Nigel that night and going to Morocco. I thought about Stacey, my father and the Dutchman's offer. I found a tapas bar on a back street. It was larger than the one where I had taken Marissa, with a black-and-white checkerboard floor. I sat at a table along the wall and ordered beer, fried goat cheese, bread and calamari. The pretty young waitress smiled at me as she set the plates on the table. I enjoyed the food slowly, trying to prolong my last moments of freedom before having to meet up again with Marissa.

At the hostel she was packed and ready, reading on the loveseat in the sitting room, clad in her black tights and green fatigues.

"Did you have a good day seeing the sights?"

She looked up from her book. "I was at the Prado most of the afternoon. Aren't the Goya's *amazing*?"

"I couldn't say. I've never been there."

She grimaced and let the book drop into her lap. "You've been in Madrid for three days, and you haven't bothered to visit the most important cultural attraction in the city?"

"I'm going to wash up and get my stuff."

When I returned fifteen minutes later she said nothing, but just stood and started walking toward the door with her backpack. We said goodbye to Señor Augusto, who had appeared from one of the adjoining rooms.

"I'll see you in a few weeks," I told him. "Next time, I'd like a room with a view."

The old man smiled and shook my hand. "See you then, Señor Clark."

With our gear Marissa and I could barely squeeze inside the tiny elevator. We stood with our bodies close together and our faces inches apart. I could feel her warmth and smell her fresh scent.

"Are you excited about seeing Tammy?"

"Oh, yeah, totally!" she said. "I can't *wait* to see her."

"Let's walk down to the plaza. It'll be easier to find a cab."

It was dusk and the cafés and bars were loud with music and laughter. The opera house shone white under electric flood lights. We found a taxi and crammed our bags into the trunk. In the back seat Marissa and I were pressed together again but still avoided one another's eyes. The cab careened through the streets, past people and traffic. Colored lights blurred inches from our windows as we sped down an alley and then whipped through the circle and dropped into a brightly lit tunnel before emerging onto a wide avenue.

At the train station the taxi driver stopped in a chaotic circular drive. People were shouting and hustling past as porters hoisted bags in and out of the cars. I paid the driver and we walked through high open doors into a bright cavernous space with a four-story ceiling. People hurried in all directions with their bags. Boarding announcements boomed from loudspeakers. Following the red letters of the electric signs we found a row of ticket windows for routes to the south. There were at least twenty people ahead of us in the line.

Tammy Whitely and Nigel Geary were set to arrive from Lisbon at any moment. While we waited I began compulsively turning to look for her amongst the crowds churning through the station. Already tired of Marissa, I was anxious to see my friend and hoped she and Nigel would arrive before we reached the ticket window. The overnight train for Algeciras was leaving in ninety minutes, at eleven o'clock. Tammy wasn't the sort who would need to rest before jumping aboard another train. She came from a family of energetic achievers who disdained weakness.

Finally I saw Tammy and Nigel plodding toward us with their bags. It looked like they didn't see us. Tammy came ambling up lanky with wide hips, wearing faded blue jeans with a hole in one knee, black shoes and a black cotton jacket.

Her shoulder-length blond hair hung down in oily strings. Nigel was dressed almost the same, but with long black hair. I thought about how much Tammy had changed since he had first appeared a year earlier and begun reshaping her in his image. When I met Tammy at the university five years prior she was an aspiring model who would show up at parties wearing elegant outfits that revealed provocative expanses of bare skin. She was always lively and laughing, her hair clean and beautifully styled, glinting blond light. When she was still in college her wealthy mother had bought her a pair of small apartment buildings, but after graduation Tammy left the work to a property manager and now spent most of her time taking long leisure trips abroad. Nigel didn't work at all.

Marissa and I waved frantically to them from our place in the line. Finally Tammy spotted us. She smiled weakly as they walked in our direction. I was disappointed by her lack of enthusiasm and wondered what was wrong.

"Hey!" I yelled, stepping forward to throw my arms around Tammy. "How are you?"

Her body tensed. "Good, Will. What's going on?"

I reached to shake Nigel's hand. "Nigel, how are you, man?"

"Aye, brilliant, brilliant, Will."

Marissa had seized Tammy and now stood between us, holding Tammy's arm and talking quickly into her ear.

"How was your trip?" I asked Nigel, still looking at Tammy.

"Not bad. Not bad. Eight hours and a bar car." He winked at me. "And you? How's Madrid?"

"It's all right. But I can't wait to get down to Morocco." My words must have sounded hollow but he didn't seem to notice.

Nigel rubbed his hands together. "It's going to be brilliant, I know. Aye, Will, there's your man." He pointed to the teller at the open window.

We bought our tickets and started walking through the station. Letters on the overhead departure and arrival signs clicked and fluttered as they spun into updated announcements.

At a kiosk I bought a ham-and-cheese sandwich and some chips and we stocked up on bottled water, cookies and orange juice. Marissa stayed at Tammy's side, monopolizing the conversation with her. I walked along with my duffel across my back, eating my sandwich in a hurry.

We found the stairway for tracks eleven and twelve. The wide stone steps curved down and as we reached the platform the long black train was waiting there, hissing and breathing heat. We walked fast, looking for number five in second class. When we found it I helped Marissa with her backpack as we climbed aboard and turned through a brief antechamber into the long tight hallway along the side of the car. We lumbered past the other sleeping compartments, bumping our bags against the walls. Some of the doors were open and I glimpsed people sitting on the seats or already starting to pull down their bunks. I walked first into our compartment; the top bunk was down on the right. Under the window there was a chrome washbasin and a heat register. Immediately I noticed the hot dry air.

"I call the bottom!" Marissa yelped, tossing her bag onto the seat on the left.

"We get the bottom on the other side!" Tammy shouted.

I chucked my bags onto the upper berth and then slid the window down on its track, opening a rectangle framed by flimsy curtains. The platforms were loud with trains clanging and blowing.

After a few minutes a man in a blue uniform arrived to take our tickets and passports. Tammy and Nigel had already stretched out on the seats below the bunk and were lying side by side. Nigel lit a cigarette. I sat by the window across from them, with Marissa next to me by the door.

"How was the horseback riding in Portugal?" I asked Tammy.

Her face brightened. "Oh, man, we had so much fun! The scenery was incredible. I rode a gorgeous mare named Liza. It was great to spend time with my mom. But some of the other ladies in the group were annoying." She made a sour face. "I got tired of being around them. Afterwards my mom flew home and Nigel came from Dublin to meet me."

The train jerked into motion, as if it had been held back and then broke free. I could feel the iron rolling and I looked out the window to see the train on the next track appear to be sliding backwards. We picked up speed and worked out of the yard into the darkness and bright colored lights of the city.

"Are you ready to smoke some hash?"

Nigel's face lit up. "Get the fuck out of here, man. Are you joking, mate?"

"Not at all. We scored last night."

Tammy looked at Marissa, who nodded to her. "It's true."

"We can't smoke hash in here!" Tammy protested.

"Why not? We'll blow it out the window."

"Yeah, I think it's all right then," Nigel said.

"At least wait until we're out of the city."

After a few minutes I reached into my bag and took out the pipe and the clump of aluminum foil. The train charged loudly down the tracks, the ties clicking in fast undulating repetition. I peeled back the foil and reached across to show the hashish to Nigel and Tammy.

"Check it out."

Her big green eyes widened and she bit her lower lip as she smiled, her face surrounded by oily blond locks. "WILL-EE-AH-NO!" Tammy bellowed comically, stretching the vowels.

Ever since she had returned from a trip to Italy the year before, she had been attaching "iano" to the ends of her friends' names. I was relieved to see Tammy being her old self again.

I tore off a corner of the gummy, sticky hashish and pressed it into the bowl.

"Can I see your lighter, Nigel?"

The smoke was thick, sweet and syrupy, like pastries baking. It expanded fast in my lungs and I coughed out a cloud that filled the compartment.

"Jeez, watch it, Williano!"

Tammy laughed loudly and then covered her mouth with her hand. We watched the smoke rush out the window in sections, as if waiting in queue. I handed the pipe and lighter to Tammy. Nigel held the flame while she puffed. Tammy immediately began coughing, leaning toward Marissa and me and then braying her nasal laugh as smoke surrounded her. We passed the pipe around and I refilled it a few times.

Nigel had a cassette player and he turned up the Rolling Stones: *"I was born in a cross-fire hurricane...."*

Outside there was only a thin curve of moon. We switched off the electric light and gray luminescence slowly spread through the compartment, glowing on any surface that faced the window. The train had left the outskirts of Madrid and was rolling south across flat countryside. Out the window I saw the headlights of a car racing us on a rural highway parallel to the tracks about a quarter mile away; in the fast distant beams I tried to glimpse what lay along the road. The side of a squat white farmhouse flashed past and then the train sped ahead and the car disappeared behind us. The hashish was kicking in strong and clean, uncluttered by alcohol this time. The rhythm of the music seemed in time with the motion of the train and Tammy and Marissa's faces were sexy and mysterious in the ghostly light. But I still missed Stacey. I wondered where she was and who she was with, what she was doing.

I climbed onto the top bunk and immediately felt the heat jump by another five or ten degrees. Lying on my back I reached into my duffel bag and found my khaki shorts. I took my jeans off over my socks, turning to let my bare legs dangle over the side in front of Tammy as I pulled on the shorts.

Marissa looked up at me. "Good idea," she said, pulling her sweater off over her head. "It's boiling in here." She was wearing a white tank top that exposed her arms and shoulders.

I jumped down and bent to inspect the radiator. There was no knob. "Isn't there any way to turn this damn thing off?"

As I stood, Nigel was suddenly next to me. He put his hands on the sides of the window and thrust his head out through the opening.

Tammy shrieked and tugged at his shoulders. "Nigel!"

A second later he pulled himself back inside. His long black hair was in his face and I couldn't see his eyes.

"It's brilliant," he laughed. "Try it!"

"Man, are you crazy? If we go through a tunnel it'll take your head off!"

"No, no, there's space, man. Just keep your mouth shut or you'll be eatin' boogs. One hit me on me cheek."

I grabbed the frame of the window and stuck my head through the open space. The sound exploded in my ears and as I turned to the left an intense rush of air pushed against my face. The long train curved with the tracks to the right, charging through the darkness; orange light hovered around its edges. I thought about the Dutchman's offer. "*It's not too late*," I told myself. A chill spread through me.

Tammy and Marissa took their turns at the window, giggling wildly. The diminutive Marissa had to step onto the heat register to reach her head through the space. Instinctively I held onto her belt.

She pulled her head back inside. "What are you doing?"

"I don't want you flying out the window." Tammy frowned at me.

There was a knock on the door. The man came into our compartment with a special wrench and lowered the other berth. Tammy and Nigel reclined under the one on their side and in the shadows their faces became darker and more abstruse. Marissa and I were hidden under the other bunk, facing the rear of the train. I watched the dark landscape flash by in reverse, broken by the far horizon above which the sky loomed only slightly lighter than the earth. The train banged and lurched. Tammy and Marissa were sharing private jokes, which they would signal with some code word before exploding in paroxysms of laughter.

After a while the buzz started to wear off and everyone looked tired. The music tape had ended and the compartment was quiet. Nigel pivoted and sat on the edge of the lower berth, bending his head down under the bunk above him. "I have a suggestion," he said. "We're going to have lots of things to pay for on this trip, and it gets too complicated to split every bill four ways. I say we all put the same amount into a kitty, and then I'll use it to pay for our taxis and meals and whatnot."

"I think it's the best system for everybody," Tammy said.

"Fine with me," Marissa agreed. "How much should we put in?"

"We won't be in Spain much longer, so maybe one thousand pesetas apiece for now, and then we'll fatten up the kitty with some Moroccan money tomorrow."

Nigel snapped on a reading light and sparse white glare spread on the wall behind their heads. I reached under my shorts into my money belt and found some bills. Nigel folded everyone's contributions and placed them into a little draw-string pouch. I noticed that he didn't add any money of his own.

"Speaking of practical matters," I said, "we really have to watch out for the guides when we get to Tangier. I've read that they offer to show you the sights, but then they rob you any way they can. They'll swarm all over us the second we step off the boat."

"Nah, it won't be a problem, man," Nigel said, waving his hand. "I can handle them."

"They've got a million tricks. One is that they take you into a carpet shop and offer you tea. But the tea is drugged, and when you come to later, you're in an alley somewhere and your wallet and your watch are both gone."

"Williano, you're freaking me out, man!"

"It's true. They also get commissions from the carpet sellers for helping extort you into buying a rug at some outrageous price. The guide leads you into a shop that's shaped like a maze, with huge carpets hanging all over the walls. When you're not looking, they roll one down over the door. Then they pressure you to buy a rug for thousands of dollars. When you tell 'em you want to leave, they say, 'Fine, go ahead.' But you can't find the door!"

"Oh, Williano, you're so high, man!" Tammy snorted her nasal laugh and threw a cookie at me.

"I'm telling you, it's true. My cousin's friend was almost forced to buy a live camel in the market in Tangier."

Marissa and Tammy laughed.

"Bollocks," Nigel said. "It'll be no different than in Mexico, where the boys were always walkin' beside Tammy and me in the streets." He cocked his head back and shook his long black hair. "You just have to know how to handle them."

"The thing we really have to be careful about is drugs," Tammy said, her tone suddenly serious. "We shouldn't buy any hash down there."

"Oh, hell no," Marissa agreed.

The stranger's face and the Dutchman's offer seeped back into my mind. I put on my hiking boots and left the compartment, trying to remain balanced as I staggered with the lurching motions of the train down the narrow corridor toward the lavatory. When I returned from the cool hallway our compartment felt ten degrees warmer, despite the open window. The room was quiet. Tammy looked like she'd already fallen asleep and Marissa was sprawled on the berth across from her. I climbed onto the top bunk. My nose was a foot from the ceiling. The air was hot and thick. "Shit, I'll never be able to sleep." Reaching into my bag I felt around for my little flashlight and shone it on my watch: twelve-thirty a.m. The train was scheduled to arrive at the port of Algeciras on Spain's southern coast at eight o'clock.

The compartment heaved as the train charged down the tracks. My legs were too long for me to stretch out; I had to either keep my knees bent or hang my feet over the side. A couple of times during the long night I started to fall asleep, only to be jolted awake as the train thudded to a stop in some obscure town.

Chapter Eight

WHEN THE TRAIN REACHED ALGECIRAS the next morning, Marissa, Nigel and I were pale and puffy-eyed from not sleeping. Only Tammy had slept well.

We stepped down onto the platform and Marissa grimaced as she adjusted the heavy pack on her back. Unlike the bustling station in Madrid this one had just a few tracks under a lower ceiling. We followed the platform to a small lobby with yellow walls. The signs were in Arabic.

Outside the morning was clear and bright. A warm breeze brushed my skin. I was exhausted but thrilled by the sea air.

"I think it's only a few blocks to the port," I said. "We can walk."

Marissa glowered at me. "Screw that, we're taking a cab."

With our gear the four of us barely fit into the tiny sedan. Marissa, Nigel and Tammy squeezed into the back seat together and I sat up front with the driver. As we pulled away and started through the town, the giant rock by the edge of the water came into view out the front window. It looked like the stump of a massive gray tree trunk.

"Check it out," I said. "The Rock of Gibraltar."

From the back seat Tammy leaned forward excitedly for a better view. "Wow, I had no idea we would see that!"

The side of the rock facing us was orange in the early

light. The north face fell away gray in shadow.

"Do you know about the apes?"

"They're baboons, Nigel," I said.

"What apes?" Tammy asked.

"The purple-assed baboons of Gibraltar. They run wild all over the rock. They'll jump on you screeching, and rip your face right off."

"You're so full of shit, Will!"

The taxi wound through the streets past little white buildings bright in the sun. The streets were mostly empty and there was something peaceful and reassuring in seeing long blank stretches of sunny pavement between the few cars that were about, their drivers in no hurry. We reached a corner where a sidewalk café had a red-and-white-striped awning emblazoned with the Coca-Cola logo in its curvy cursive script. A few people were sitting there drinking coffee and reading the morning papers. The traffic light changed and the driver turned onto a one-way street paved with bricks; on either side there were empty lots sprouting weeds. The street led down to the dock where the ferry was waiting. I could see the sun shining on the water.

When the taxi reached the ferry terminal Nigel paid the driver while I helped Tammy and Marissa with their bags. The building was three stories high and on the first floor there was a galleria of ticket booths for the boat operators. They competed for customers with colorful signs offering fares to Tangier, Ceuta and other points around the Mediterranean. Past the galleria there was a corridor lined with storage lockers.

"We should stash anything we don't need for Morocco," Nigel said.

We filled two lockers with our belongings. I left the pipe and the remaining hashish, along with a book I had finished and some souvenirs from Madrid. Tammy filled almost an entire locker with her knickknacks from Portugal.

With our burdens lightened we walked to the ticket windows and found the ferry to "Tanger." The signs were in Arabic, Spanish, English and French.

"The next one leaves at eleven," Nigel said. "That's in two-and-a-half hours."

We purchased our second-class tickets and found a shop where we bought sandwiches and pastries. We ate our breakfasts outside on concrete benches. Along the shore the mountains of Andalusia were hazy in the early glare. Sweet sea scent mixed with the stench of diesel exhaust from buses arriving to drop off passengers.

Marissa prattled on to Tammy as I studied a map of Tangier. "The train station is only a few blocks from the port," I said to Nigel. "We can take a cab or walk."

After a couple of hours we rode an escalator to the second floor, where we presented our tickets at a counter and then walked down a long covered ramp to the dock outside. A small crowd was forming. Many of the passengers were Arab men, some wearing fezzes or skullcaps. Sitting on their bags were a thin young white man with bleached blond hair and a chubby girl with black hair. "Look at the fag hag," Tammy said. "That is too funny." Marissa laughed, eagerly going along. "The guides are going to eat those two alive," I thought to myself.

Finally the gate opened and the passengers started moving up the gangplank. Excitement and fear ran through me. I knew it still wasn't too late to turn back, but felt myself being pulled one step closer.

In a crowded anteroom inside the ferry we waited in line to check our bags, and then passed through a short corridor into the main cabin. There was a dark wood bar in the center; toward the stern, a restaurant with tables and chairs. Nearer the bow was a lounge with overstuffed orange-vinyl furniture along the windows.

We bought drinks and walked outside onto the deck. A half hour later the ferry began moving through the harbor and into the Strait of Gibraltar. The water and sky were the deepest blue I had ever seen, covered by a curtain of drifting mist. I leaned on the railing in the fresh windy sunshine. Infinite whitecaps were bursting on the blue water and seagulls floated like white confetti through the spray. In the distance giant freighters were heading for the Atlantic, their outlines blurred by the airborne sheets of gossamer droplets. Nigel and Marissa were taking pictures. The North African coast was only eight miles away, but the ride would take three hours as the ferry worked westward through the strait toward Tangier.

After a while we walked to the stern, where a sudsy wake churned white through the blue behind the boat. Schools of dolphins rode the waves. In groups of three or four they would burst up through the surf, shining wet in the sun for an instant, appearing suspended in air, before plunging back down into the water. In the distance to starboard the green hills of Spain were hazy in shadow; to port sun lit the gray cliffs of Africa.

A couple of hours later, after we had eaten lunch, we were half-asleep on the orange furniture when a man in a gray uniform appeared and sat at a chair behind a long table.

"Aye," Nigel said. "There's your man."

A line formed and the official began checking the passengers' passports and entry forms. He had a stern demeanor and wore glasses, a heavy moustache and a constant frown. His black hat had a shiny rim, and there was a colorful crest on his uniform with the flag of Morocco. We would also have to submit our carry-on bags for inspection. I wondered if someone was looking through the bags we had checked, and tried to remember what was still in my duffel and what I had left in the locker in Spain.

When I reached the front of the line I set my passport and canvas satchel on the table. Without altering his dour expression the official thumbed past stamps from the Caribbean, South America and Europe, lingering on a recent stamp from Schiphol Airport in Amsterdam. He flipped backwards through the pages and when he reached my photograph at the front he looked up at me with heavy humorless eyes. The black-and-white photograph had been shot in a studio and showed me dressed in a jacket and tie. I must have looked quite different to him now, unshaven, my hair longer and in a mess, wearing jeans, a blue T-shirt and a pea-green jacket. The official removed a couple of paperback books and a map from my satchel and then peered into the bottom and poked through my reporters' notebooks and pens. He looked at me again and then turned past several blank pages in my passport. On the last page he stamped an entry visa for Tangier.

It was about two in the afternoon when the town came into view. We stood on the deck and watched as the ferry drew closer. Little white cube houses were stacked across a series of hills. Four-sided minarets towered over the roofs. Higher up the mountain mansions looked over the town. The dreamlike sight belied the dread I felt but the possibility that I could still back out gave me fleeting rushes of hope.

Tammy was biting her lower lip. "I can't believe we're almost there." I looked at Marissa and was surprised to see her grinning at me.

PART II

Chapter Nine

THE NIGHT OF THE KILLINGS I heard Tammy and Nigel crying in their sleep on the train. I dreamt of Marissa squatting naked in black stiletto heels, masturbating with the switchblade as big round drops of blood and cum dripped out of her onto the floor. Her face twisted with pleasure and pain. Tammy was lying naked next to Marissa, rubbing herself with her fingertips. Milk oozed from her nipples, forming into bubbles that floated up into the air and then popped. Somewhere in the background Nigel was sobbing and vomiting. The dying faces of Fareed and his friends floated through the gray periphery of my dream.

We had bribed the man on the train to accept the irregularity in our tickets, as I had hoped we could. When I woke in the morning Marissa was lying beside me with her arm across my chest. She and the others were still asleep. The sky was beginning to lighten. It was just past dawn when the train reached Rabat. When they woke my companions were quiet and morose, like people preparing for a funeral.

I sucked in my breath as Marissa and I stepped down onto the platform together, ahead of Tammy and Nigel. Looking around I expected to see rows of policemen waiting for us. But there was just one man in a uniform standing on the far end of the platform, and I wasn't sure whether he was even a policeman. Most of the disembarking passengers were Moroccans, men in long robes or veiled women with small children. There were a few Europeans in business suits and a group of blond students carrying backpacks. Everyone seemed tired.

I was on guard but confident, and it seemed by her outward demeanor that Marissa felt the same way. She seemed to still be pretending we were a couple on a lark. I was surprised by my own lack of emotion, but knew instinctively not to question it. To Tammy and Nigel I had framed as a practical matter the idea of splitting into pairs, a strategy to throw off anyone looking for a group of four. But the truth was that I didn't trust Tammy or her boyfriend and was afraid they would betray us with their skittish behavior. If anything happened I was prepared to leave them behind.

The station lobby was tiled in white and blue and there was a four-foot-high photograph of the king above the double exit doors. His Majesty smiled down paternally, wearing glasses and a dark suit. Arabic script curled across the bottom of the portrait.

Marissa and I walked out to a circular drive where two taxis were waiting in the early sun. In the center of the turnaround stood a tall palm tree ringed with yellow and purple flowers. Their thick powdery scent was on the air. The sun felt good.

A porter asked in French where we wanted to go.

"L'Hotel Tunis, si'l vous plait."

He seemed surprised. "Are you sure, monsieur?"

"Yes. Thank you."

On the train Tammy and Nigel had nodded with downcast eyes to my suggestion for another evasive tactic, that as two pairs we would take taxis to other hotels before meeting at the Splendide.

Now Marissa lowered her sunglasses and looked at me.

In the direct light I could distinguish tiny round pupils from her dark irises. The corners of her mouth curled up.

"You seem to know your way around," she said.

The driver got out and opened the rear taxi door for us. The car was a Mercedes sedan, a utilitarian model but spacious. I tipped the porter and after loading our luggage into the trunk the driver looped the taxi through the driveway and onto a wide boulevard. Over Marissa's shoulder I could see Tammy and Nigel coming out of the station, surrounded by the student travelers. Tammy was smiling her broad toothy smile, long strands of blond hair over her eyes. Nigel looked pale as he limped with his bag. The boulevard median was landscaped with palm trees and rose bushes; on either side white buildings with French architecture shone amber in the nascent sun, low behind us as we rode toward the medina. A rectangular minaret stood over the town and in a park orange trees displayed bright yields. A breeze blew through the open windows of the taxi and I could smell the clean scent of the Atlantic. For a moment I allowed myself to feel refreshed. The driver turned at a traffic light and we were on a narrow street between rows of short apartment buildings. Only a few people were out. I saw a vendor at a corner fruit stand and asked the driver to stop.

Marissa smiled and the sun reflected off her dark sunglasses. I could see grease on the lenses in little rainbow streaks. The morning light was soft over her face, and her teeth and lips looked moist.

"I'll stay in the car," she said. "But buy me some oranges, will you, Darling?"

The man standing amongst the produce smiled as I approached him. I was choosing some oranges and dates when I saw a police car pass behind us at the end of the block. My heart quickened. I paid the vendor and got back into the taxi.

After a few more turns and traffic lights the driver stopped near a rounded portal in the medina wall. "The Tunis is just inside to the right," he said, turning to look at me. "But are you certain you want to stay at this hotel, monsieur?"

"Sure, why not?"

"This is a dirty hotel. Bad people. My uncle has a better place near the Kasbah, nice clean rooms, private terraces over the sea. Not expensive."

"Sounds beautiful, but perhaps another time. How much do I owe you?"

"This hotel is not for the Americans."

"We're Canadian."

I paid the driver and Marissa and I got out and started walking with our bags. The native quarter began behind the crumbling gray rampart walls. We passed under the gate; inside there were rows of shop stalls on a crooked little street. An alleyway barely wider than my shoulders followed the inside of the wall. Past a few nondescript doorways the hotel's small sign said in block letters: TUNIS. Sunlight reached the upper part of the wall but where we were walking the alley was damp in shadow. The door of the hotel was open and I could see a flight of wooden stairs that rose and turned to the left. The cramped space smelled musty.

Just then a man came down the steps.

"You are looking for a room?"

Marissa gasped. He stared at her with one eye. The other was milky white.

"No, sorry," I said. "My mistake."

"Come, I have a good room for you."

We walked away, back to where the driver had left us at the mouth of the medina. A butcher had opened his shutters and was standing over a table stacked with goat heads. The animals' esophagi stuck out below their severed necks and their eyes stared dead glazed. They seemed to be smiling.

The butcher looked at us expressionlessly, using a stick to swat away the flies. Old women in the alleys were arranging baskets of fruits and vegetables over blankets spread on the ground. A few shoppers were starting to arrive.

A cat cried as it dashed past our feet. Stepping back through the gate in the medina wall I looked up the road and saw the police car waiting at a red light.

"Do you have your camera handy?" I said. "Why don't you get a shot of those goat heads?"

Marissa dug into her bag. The police car crossed the intersection and approached us. Marissa raised the viewfinder to her eye. I stood next to her looking at the butcher and heard the rush of cars passing behind us as the shutter flicked.

"No pictures!" the man yelled angrily in French, waving his arm.

I glanced around and saw the police car driving away. In a group of vehicles coming toward us from the other direction was a taxi's roof light. I waved for the driver to stop, and Marissa and I slid into the back seat with our bags.

After a couple of blocks the driver turned onto a wider avenue and stopped at a traffic light. Another taxi pulled alongside us. It was the one who had dropped us at the medina gate.

I turned to face Marissa and leaned forward to block the other driver's view of her. From the corner of my eye I could see our driver looking across to his colleague. They shouted to one another in Arabic. The words sounded harsh, but for what I knew they might have been talking about the weather. Finally the light changed and they started driving again. I fought the temptation to turn and look at the other man. At the next intersection our driver veered left and then a couple of blocks later turned left again.

The Hotel Splendide was on a quiet one-way street of low-rise apartments, all of them white, with a few shops and cafés. The driver got out and lifted our bags from the back seat. He seemed to look at me suspiciously as I paid him. From the sidewalk a half dozen wide steps led up to a pair of heavy glass doors. Inside, a long dark hallway extended to the rear of the hotel and there was a reception desk on the left. Fans twirled on the high ceiling. Tropical plants rose from ceramic pots on the floor.

The man at the desk found my room reservation and remarked that the hotel was filling up quickly because of an economic summit starting in the city the next day. He asked to see our passports and jotted down the numbers.

"You arrived late, monsieur. We expected you last night."

"Yes, that's my fault," I said. "I insisted we go straight to the beach when we got off the train, and we ended up falling asleep there."

The man looked at me and nodded, smiling.

A bellman took Marissa's bag and led us up the stairs to the second floor. At the first landing a light fixture was suspended from the ceiling; it projected red and orange stars and crescent moons across the ceiling and walls. The heels of the man's shoes clicked on the stone steps.

At the end of the hallway the door opened at an angle into the cool dark room. At first I couldn't see anything and then the light around the drapes seemed to brighten. The man stepped over and pulled them aside, revealing gossamer curtains. The room had two twin beds with white linens and dark end tables. The bellman snapped on the bathroom light; I tipped him and he left.

"Well, we made it."

"And the first thing on my list is to take a long, hot shower," Marissa said. "I don't think I've ever needed one more badly before in my life."

"I should go downstairs to look for them."

"Do you think they're coming?"

"Don't you?"

"I'm not sure," she said.

"Why?"

"Maybe Tammy will decide to find a different hotel. Or they'll go straight to the airport."

"Tammy's smarter than that, I hope."

"She better be." Marissa stripped to her underwear, took her bag into the bathroom and shut the door.

Below the window the courtyard had a small fountain and an arrangement of wrought-iron furniture, shaded by a tree. Behind it was a coach house with a door, on the second floor an open pair of green shutters against a canary-yellow wall. Pajamas and nightshirts on clotheslines animated in the breeze on the flat roof, white, pastel pink and powder blue. There were just a few cirrus clouds in the sky.

I could hear the water running. "I'm going downstairs to look for them," I said through the bathroom door.

"Will, no, don't leave while I'm still in the shower!"

I took off my socks and shirt and lay back on the bed nearest the bathroom door, and then peeled an orange and bit into the delicious fruit. We hadn't turned on any lamps and the room was still dark and cool. The ceiling fan spun languidly. I must have been drifting to sleep when light from the bathroom suddenly shone on my eyes. The door was open and Marissa was standing in front of the mirror wearing only a cream-colored towel around her body. Her legs were bare from the thighs down. "Your turn," she said, stepping out of the bathroom and looking at me as I went in and closed the door. I used the toilet and then got into the shower. The water was hot, with strong pressure, and I stood gratefully under the showerhead, feeling my neck and shoulders relax. The soap had a sandalwood scent. It was my first shower in two days and I took my time washing my face and hair and body. But then creeping into the physical pleasure came threatening thoughts about what I had done, and about the Dutchman. As if through a churning black cloud I saw the faces of Stacey and my dad. A fantasy brightened my mind: I'm introducing them to each other—everyone's smiling and laughing and we're eating steaks at Gene & Georgetti, and maybe I'll propose to her after dinner. And then it drifted away.

When I stepped out of the shower the bathroom door was slightly ajar. Standing over the sink I splashed hot water on my face and neck and spread shaving cream over my two-day growth of beard. I let the cream soak in while I brushed back my wet hair. I shaved slowly. The gurgling sound of the razor rinsing through the hot water in the sink seemed loud in the silent room.

I was drying my neck with a hand towel when the bathroom door slowly opened farther. Marissa was still wearing the towel. She tilted her head to one side and smiled, wrapping one bare leg around the other. Her eyes moved over my chest and down to my waist.

"How'd you get that bruise on your hip, Will?"

"Oh, I don't know. Must've banged into a wall or something."

"Nice silk boxers," she giggled. "Red paisley, no less."

"Do you like them?"

"Where on Earth did you buy underpants like that?"

"They were a gift."

"I have a present for you, too."

Marissa took a couple of steps backward toward the bed, looking me in the eye. She dropped the towel. For the first time I saw her naked body, sinuous with small round breasts, tiny pink areolas and nipples erect with life. Her skin was creamy and glowing, swirling around her navel, and she stood with her legs bent shyly to one side, but I could see a patch of brown hair between them. I pulled down the waistband of my boxers and stepped naked toward Marissa. She looked at me and opened her mouth. I lifted her petit body off the floor and laid her back on the bed, spreading her open. She tasted sweet and sour, slightly stinging my taste buds. She whimpered through the silence.

I moved forward onto my knees. Marissa looked at it and huffed and then hissed as she inhaled through clenched teeth. She reached forward with her open lips, filling them as she met me. I had discovered secret treasure in that cool dark room, and a flooding sense of liberation. I lifted her off the bed and went inside her. Our moans sounded amplified as we stood fucking in the quiet.

"You wanted this before, didn't you, baby?" she said.

"Yeah."

"I knew you did, and I wanted it, too … Oh, Will, I love it! Do you love it, baby?"

I didn't say anything, and she slapped me.

"Yeah, okay, yeah, I love it." I thrust into her harder and she gasped.

"You know what else I've wanted you to do to me? Huh?"

"What?"

"Put me on the bed again," she panted.

Marissa turned over onto her knees and elbows. Her body shook and she turned her head and bit at the air. I felt the climax coming twenty heartbeats before it arrived. My mind and body seemed to drift apart as each beat thumped closer, and when the wave that I was sure would be the one finally seemed about to crest, time slowed torturously. My pulse thudded but I was still suspended over the edge. With the next heaving undulation pleasure crashed through me; Marissa was shuddering and I felt myself passing out, falling to one side, out of my body.

Chapter Ten

SOMETIME LATER I was awakened by a knock on the door. Marissa was asleep next to me, still naked. Another knock. I stood up and pulled on my trousers, and then walked over to crack open the door. It was the bellman.

"Forgive the intrusion, monsieur, but there is a visitor here to see you. I tried ringing your room, but there was no answer."

"Who is it?"

"A young lady. She is waiting for you in the lobby."

"I'll be down in five minutes. Thank you."

It was mid-morning but the stairwell was still dark and the colored stars and crescent moons shone on my clothes. At the last landing I heard a familiar voice. She was standing with her back to me, talking to the man. Her blond hair was too long. She turned and I saw that it was Stacey Snow.

"Will, there you are!" She ran over and threw her arms around me.

I was a little stunned, and for a few seconds just stood there looking at her, not knowing what to say. "Stacey, how are you?" I squeezed her body against mine. "When did you arrive in Rabat?"

"I got here last night," she said, a smile lighting up her face. "I remembered you said you'd be staying at this hotel."

She looked at me. "Are you okay?"

"Yeah, yeah, I'm fine. Just so surprised to see you. Do you have a room here?"

"No, I'm at the Excelsior, near the American Embassy. When did you get here?"

The man behind the counter glanced up at me.

"Just a couple hours ago."

"Well, I'm going out to see the ruins this afternoon," she said. "Wanna tag along? That is, if Marissa will allow it. She's here with you, right?"

"Sleeping upstairs."

Stacey raised her eyebrows. "You're sharing a room?"

"Just to save money. It's got two beds."

She tossed her hair back and took a couple of steps toward a rack of tourist leaflets, running her fingertips over them absently. Down the hall there was a loveseat and I led her to it.

"How did you come to Rabat?" I asked her.

Stacey was avoiding my eyes. "I flew from Seville."

"Did you have any trouble?"

She looked at me. "With what?"

"With the guides, the hustlers."

"Oh, there were a few at the airport, and around the cabstands. But they were nothing I couldn't handle."

"It's not as bad in Rabat," I said, "since the king is here."

Just then, over Stacey's shoulder, I saw Tammy and Nigel walk in through the glass doors, lugging their bags. He was still limping.

"I missed you that morning in Madrid," I said. "What happened to you?"

She looked away from my eyes. "Oh, I was worried about missing my train, so I left early … But then I started thinking about what you said, about coming to Morocco, and what a magical place it's supposed to be, and all that. Anyway, I thought we could have lunch together today and then head out to see the ruins."

"The storks make their nests on top of the ruined pillars and arches," I said. "You can see the big white birds up close."

Stacey looked at me with a surprised, quizzical expression. "Storks? I hadn't heard about them … Does that mean you're coming with me, Will?"

"I would love to. Just wait here for me, and I'll be back down in ten minutes."

I kissed her. She looked at me with her blue eyes, but her expression seemed troubled. The tip of her tongue went around her lips and I wondered if she tasted Marissa on my mouth. "Okay," she said.

As I was walking to the stairs Tammy saw me.

"All the hotels are full," I heard the man behind the desk saying. "But you are in luck. We just received a cancellation."

Nigel looked pale and disheveled, and didn't seem to notice me passing behind them.

"Two-oh-three," I whispered.

In the room Marissa was sitting up in bed, still naked, eating an orange.

"We need some fresh air in here," I said, pushing open the window. More light shone into the room.

"What's going on?"

"Tammy and Nigel are downstairs, checking in."

"She asked for us?"

"No."

"But I heard the man say a young lady was here."

"That wasn't Tammy."

"What? Who was it, then?"

"Stacey, a girl I met in Madrid."

"You're kidding me."

"She's downstairs. I was talking to her when Tammy and Nigel came in. We're going out to see the ruins together."

Marissa's face darkened. "Darling, you must be joking."

"Darling?"

"You're with me now."

There was a soft knock at the door. Shadows played across the frosted glass of the transom.

"Who is it?"

Another gentle knock. Marissa was dressing and I turned back the deadbolt and opened the door an inch. Tammy's green eyes looked at me in the dim light.

"Christ, where have you been?" Marissa said as Tammy and Nigel walked into the room.

"We went for breakfast," Nigel said, looking away from Marissa and me. It was hard to imagine either of them gathering the composure to eat in a restaurant.

"Did you go to the Hotel Muniria, like we talked about?" I asked him.

"No, we came straight here after we ate," Tammy said. She looked at the tossed sheets on the bed and made a sour face. "My God, what's that smell?"

"That was almost two hours ago," I said, looking at my watch.

"We took our time." Tammy and Nigel stood close to each other near an armoire along the wall, on the other side of the bed from Marissa and me.

"Did you have any trouble?" Marissa asked them.

"No trouble," Nigel said. "Not yet. But I don't want to stay here long."

"We just have to clean ourselves up," Tammy said. "And then we should go."

"What did you tell those students?" Marissa's voice was

ugly. "Did you say we'd been to the fishing village?"

"You must think I'm a damned idiot!" Tammy yelled at her.

"Well, I know how friendly you are with strangers."

"Look, you two can do what you bloody well like," Nigel said, "but Tammy and I are flying back to Lisbon immediately, and from there we'll get the first plane to the States."

"No. You'd be crazy to go to the airport."

"Marissa is right," I said. "Think about it: You arrive by ferry in Tangier yesterday afternoon, you take the train to Rabat, and now the next morning you're boarding a plane back to Europe? It's going to look suspicious."

"All right then, smart guy," Tammy said to me. "Have you got a better idea?"

"We can hire a boat to take us back to Spain. We'll find some fisherman we can pay cash, no questions. We'll go tonight."

The room was silent as the four of us stood looking at each other.

"And you think we can find a boat," Tammy said, "just like that?"

"It's worth a try. You three should stay here and lay low. Right now I'm going with a friend to see the ruins, and then I'll try to line up a boat."

Tammy was livid. "What *friend*?!"

"A girl he fucked in Madrid," Marissa said. "She's waiting for him downstairs."

Tammy's face was red. "The one you were talking to in the lobby?"

"Her name is Stacey. I met her at the pensión."

"And you're going out *sightseeing* with this girl, Clark? Are you out of your damn mind?!"

Nigel touched Tammy's arm. "No, that's okay, let him go. You go ahead with her, man. We'll stay here. That's all right."

"But Will," Marissa said, "why let the cops see you?"

"They're all busy with this trade summit. And there are other young travelers around. We have to act like nothing's wrong."

Marissa's eyes were hard. "All right, but your bags stay here."

"What do you care?" Tammy snapped. She looked again at the tossed bedding.

Marissa glared back at her. "You just worry about Nigel."

It probably was a bad idea for me to go see the ruins with Stacey. I didn't want to put her in danger. But my attraction to her was growing into something far stronger than what I had felt in Madrid. She was no longer just an object of my physical or even emotional desire. She had become my hope. I wanted to see her, and to be free from these others who I was sure would only cause my destruction. I reasoned to myself that I needed to protect Stacey now that she had asked for me at the hotel and the man at the desk had seen us together.

But when I reached the lobby, she was gone.

OUTSIDE IT WAS SUNNY AND HOT. As I had done in Madrid I looked up and down the street but did not see Stacey. I should have been relieved. Instead my heart sank into my guts.

Up the block there was a corner café. Chairs and small round tables jumbled onto the sidewalk, shaded by a canvas awning. The air smelled of coffee and cigarette smoke. An old gentleman was sitting alone at a table in the back. He looked European, with wavy blond hair streaked gray at the temples, dressed in a sand-colored suit with a white dress shirt open at the collar.

I sat at a table and ordered tea and a croissant. A young Moroccan woman walked past wearing a business suit and low-heeled shoes, hair uncovered but tied back. Every few minutes some miniature European car would zip past, or a motorcycle or scooter, but there was very little traffic on the street. It was approaching noon and the sun was severe with no lateral shadows. I found a copy of *The International Herald Tribune* and read the headlines. The waiter poured my tea into a glass stuffed with mint leaves and sugar. On the radio a woman began singing a French ballad.

The man behind me cleared his throat. "It's a terrible thing, isn't it?"

I turned to look at him. "Her voice?"

He laughed. "No, I mean the story there in the paper. People butchering their neighbors. It's a horror. Shouldn't mankind be past such barbarity by now?"

There was an article on the front page of the *Herald* about militias hacking people to death in Algeria.

"Where do you suppose this savagery comes from?" he said.

"Maybe it's man's reaction to his disappointment in himself, his fear that others will discover the truth about him."

The man pushed back his chair and stood, and then stepped over to me and extended his hand. "Geiler. Arnaud Geiler." He smelled of smoke and bay rum.

"Will Clark, nice to meet you, Mister Geiler."

He offered me one of his Dunhill's.

"No thanks. Don't smoke."

Geiler sat down across from me. His eyes were gray blue and his face was lined but tan. He lit a new cigarette and the smoke slipped from the shade into the caustic light.

"You are American?"

"Yes, from Chicago."

He smiled. "How do you like Morocco?"

"It's a wondrous place."

"First time in Rabat?"

"Third."

Just then a police car turned onto the street. The sun

glared silver off the windshield and I couldn't see the driver's face. He seemed to slow down as he passed the hotel. My stomach tightened.

"I thought you looked familiar," Geiler said. "Have we talked before?"

"Not that I can remember. But you might have seen me around."

"I spend all day in these cafés, so I see everyone in Rabat."

"You're retired?"

The police car passed the café and stopped at the curb.

"Yes, after thirty-five years of importing condensed milk. The company is in Brussels. I ran the office here, and my wife Saskia and I had a house in the ville nouveau. She's gone now."

A policeman in sunglasses and a gray uniform stepped into the light. He waved to the proprietor, who shouted to him in Arabic.

"I'm sorry about your wife. You must miss her."

"Very much, yes."

"Do you like to be retired?"

"It's a lonely life now," Geiler said, hissing smoke. "But I still do an occasional bit of consulting on how to conduct business here in Morocco." He knocked ash into a glass tray on the table. "And you, Mister Clark? What is your métier?"

The policeman glanced at me as he walked to the counter.

"I write articles."

"A correspondent?"

"In a sense, yes."

"Which publications do you write for?"

"The Chicago Today is my main paper, but most of my feature stories also get syndicated to other newspapers around the country or abroad. I write for some magazines in New York, too."

"Then you are here to cover the summit, I assume?"

"Just a couple of short dispatches. I'm mostly writing about leisure travel on this trip. Hotels and restaurants, things like that."

The policeman was drinking coffee and talking to the man behind the counter but he seemed to be listening to me, too.

"This country would not survive without tourism," Geiler said. "Have you been to Fez? There are some wonderful hotels there for you to write about."

"Yes, once before. And I'm going again in a few days."

I watched the policeman from the edge of my eye. He seemed to be looking at me, but it was hard to tell with his dark glasses.

"Traveling in Morocco can be complicated," Geiler said, reaching into his jacket and bringing out a brown leather sheath. "Trouble is easy to find, if you know what I mean. If you have any problems, I might be able to help." He handed me a card.

"I would give you one of mine, but they're back at my hotel."

"Staying nearby?"

"No, on the cheap in the medina, I'm afraid."

Geiler looked at me and smiled oddly. I thought I saw his eyes flick to the policeman.

"I can't imagine you writing about any of the hotels down there," he said. "Nasty conditions, if you ask me."

"The place is colorful, that's for sure," I chuckled. "But sometimes dives are where you find the most interesting stories. I remember one time in Costa Rica, turned out this dumpy hotel was also a whorehouse. Made good copy. Anyway, it's just for a couple of nights in the medina. I'll be much more comfortable in a few days, at the Palais Jamai in Fez."

The old man's eyes brightened. "Now there is a beautiful

hotel," he said. "Saskia and I stayed there many times."

I had finished my snack and tea. I dropped a couple coins on the table and rose to leave. "It was nice to meet you, Mister Geiler."

"Likewise, Mister Clark. Please do not hesitate to call."

The policeman turned to look at me, no doubt about it this time. I walked away from the café and the hotel, circling several blocks before slipping through the glass doors, up the dark stairway and into its galaxy of stars and moons.

Chapter Eleven

MARISSA WAS READING in bed. "Back from seeing the ruins already?"

"I decided not to go."

She perked up. "Really? Why not?"

"Too risky, like you said."

"Where's Stacey?"

"She went alone."

The smug grin made Marissa's face ugly. "Well, it's really too bad that your plans with her didn't work out." She stood from the bed and walked over to put her arms behind my neck. "The ruins do sound interesting, though. Maybe we should visit them together?" She kissed me on the mouth, but I pulled back.

"No, I think it's best to stay close to the others now," I said. "But I'm hungry. I'm going out to find some lunch, if you'd like to come."

ON THE SIDEWALK in front of the hotel we turned to the right, in the opposite direction from the café where I had met Geiler. It was afternoon and the sunlight had tilted; our side of the street was hot and bright and our shadows followed us along the walls. I looked around and didn't see any policemen. I knew I should have been worried but I just didn't feel it. Whatever was going to happen would happen. Marissa appeared insouciant, and I couldn't tell if it was just an act. Looking at her and seeing our reflections in the windows I realized that both our appearances had changed. For the first time since we had met in Spain, she was not dressed in her usual tomboy clothes. The olive-green headscarf was gone. She was still wearing her black, wedge-heeled sandals, but now her toenails were freshly painted. She must have done that while I was in the café. Designer jeans fit tight around her curves. She wore a white V-neck top with a black sweater draped over her back, the sleeves tied across her chest. Even Marissa's hair looked different, combed down and curled forward from her ears. A loop shone in the light against the soft flesh of her jaw. I saw myself in beige cotton-linen pants, collared white shirt, brown leather shoes. We were both wearing sunglasses.

At the road outside the medina walls a procession of black sedans was speeding past, dark windows reflecting sun. Little flags snapped from the antennae and the cars were surrounded by policemen on motorcycles. I wondered if the king might be in one of the limousines. I looked around for Stacey, but didn't see her anywhere.

Crossing the avenue we came to the ramparts and passed under a gateway into the medina. Old men in fezzes and long robes stood near the entrance and shuffled among the rows of cluttered stalls. Women floated by, hidden in haiks and veils. The air smelled of sea water, raw meat and fish. In the background the Atlantic shone blue and silver above the white parapet.

We found a small restaurant and sat inside by the window. The waiter smiled as he handed us menus. Marissa and I sipped mineral water while we waited for our warm fig salads and lamb tagine.

"You don't seem worried," I said.

She smiled falsely and shrugged her shoulders. "It doesn't seem real. It was just a bad dream."

Her denial had the opposite effect on me, clarifying the weight of our predicament. It made me resent her more but I didn't want to upset her carefree demeanor. I forced myself to change the subject.

"Let me ask you something. Why do you think Tammy has been so hostile on this trip? Her whole attitude has changed since the last time I saw her in Chicago."

"She's looking for someone to blame for her stupid mistake last night."

"Yeah, but I mean before, when we met them at the train station in Madrid. She didn't seem happy to see us."

Marissa gazed absently at people passing the window. "She was probably jealous to see us together."

I always doubted any hypothesis that flattered me. "That can't be it," I said. "Tammy and I are friends. And she knows that you and I don't get along."

"It doesn't matter if you're just friends. She can still be jealous."

"It doesn't make sense."

"You obviously don't understand women."

"You got that right."

"But as it's turned out, she was right to be jealous about us, right baby?" She reached across the table to touch my hand.

"What about Nigel? Do you think she really loves him? She keeps telling me to save my money for an Irish wedding."

Marissa smirked. "Please, that loser? She's just slumming with him to punish her rich parents. It won't last, believe me. Especially now. Of course, your friendship with Tammy has no future, either, even though you saved her stupid ass."

"Why do you say that?"

"You were brave, and her cocky boyfriend almost pissed himself. Do you think she's ever going to forgive you for that?"

A ceiling fan spun quietly over our heads. There was only one other diner in the restaurant, a man sitting alone and staring at a soccer game on a little television on the white-tile counter. The waiter brought our food and Marissa and I started eating.

"Do you think they were really at breakfast for two hours this morning?"

Marissa looked at me. "It seems hard to believe, doesn't it? They're a couple of basket cases. Nigel would run from his own shadow."

WE WALKED BACK to the main road and found a taxi. I had the driver stop in front of a building two blocks from the hotel, and we waited for him to drive away before walking around the corner toward the Splendide.

And there was Geiler. He seemed happy to see me.

"Why, Mister Clark, how is everything?" He looked at Marissa, grinning expectantly.

"Hello again, Mister Geiler, how are you? I'd like you to meet Marissa."

"Pleased to meet you, mademoiselle," he said, bowing slightly.

"Hello."

"We've just been to lunch in the native quarter. It looks like the diplomats have started to arrive."

"Oh yes, the whole town is coming alive now. Exciting, isn't it?"

A taxi turned up the street and stopped near us. The driver was the one who had picked us up at the train station that morning. "Hey, Canadian! You need a ride somewhere?"

Geiler looked at me and then at the driver. "Hello, Ali,"

he said.

"Bon jour, monsieur Geiler," the driver said, and then yelled at me: "Is the Tunis not dirty, as I told you? Come with me, I will drive you and your bride to the hotel of my uncle, beautiful view of the sea!"

"No, thanks."

He waved his hand and continued up the street.

"Sometimes it's easier to tell the Arabs we're Canadian. We don't have to hear as many diatribes."

"I cannot remember another time when people around the world have held such a favorable view of America," Geiler said.

"Sometimes people are jealous."

"Of course, Miss—or should I say, 'Mrs. Clark?'"

I laughed. "We're not married."

Marissa hooked her elbow around mine and pulled her body against me. "Not yet, anyway."

"Well then, Mister Clark will have to propose to you very soon, mademoiselle. Perhaps in Fez?"

"Yeah, maybe in Fez," I laughed, squeezing Marissa's arm.

"We'll see," she said, looking up at me with surprise.

From over Geiler's shoulder I saw Tammy and Nigel leaving the Splendide and walking toward us. "Well, we should be going," I said. "It's been nice chatting with you again, Mister Geiler."

"Yes, and for me, as well. Remember, do not hesitate to call if there is anything I can do for you. I know everyone in Rabat."

"Do you know someone with a boat we can charter?" Marissa blurted.

Geiler looked surprised. "Why yes, in fact I do."

"I don't think we'll have time," I said. "C'mon, we'd better head over to the conference. See you around, Mister Geiler."

"Until next time, Mister Clark. It was nice meeting you,

young lady."

We took a couple of steps and found ourselves facing Tammy and Nigel.

"Where have you been?" Tammy hissed.

"Oh, hello," I said, continuing past them.

"Are you going back to the Splendide?"

"We're staying in the native quarter," I said. "We'll see you later."

When we reached the corner I glanced back. Tammy and Nigel were talking to Geiler. "*Goddamn them.*"

We turned toward the train station and gradually looped back to the hotel. I was watching for the policeman, expecting to see him. But it seemed that the entire force was busy escorting the motorcades. About forty minutes had passed by the time Marissa and I walked back into the hotel lobby, which was now crowded with men in suits.

We washed up in our room and then took the stairs to the next floor to look for Tammy and Nigel. At first there was no answer when I knocked. We were about to walk away when I heard Tammy's voice. The lock snapped and she opened the door. Behind her the room was dark. When we walked in I saw Nigel pacing near the window.

"What's going on?" he said. "Where's your friend? Did you see the ruins?"

"No, she decided to go alone. Marissa and I had lunch in the medina." I looked at Nigel's sallow face and long black hair. "The authorities are all busy with the trade summit. We didn't have any problems."

"We have to get *out* of here," Tammy groaned.

"The fucking cops could come crashing through the door at any minute," Nigel said.

"Relax," Marissa said. "Right after dark, we're gone."

"Did you find a boat?"

"No."

"Well, then how do you know?" Tammy demanded. "Where are we going to find one?"

"In one of the harbors," I said.

"I have a bad feeling about this," she said, biting her thumbnail. "We're just going to ask some strange man to give us a ride on his filthy boat? And we have to cross the Strait in it, for God's sake?"

"These people are poor. They'll jump at the chance to make some extra money."

"Who was that old man you were talking to outside?" Nigel asked me.

"Geiler. I met him in the café. Maybe he can help us find a boat."

"What did you say to him?" Marissa asked Nigel.

"We weren't even talking to him," Tammy said.

"Christ, Tammy," Marissa snapped. "We saw you!"

"I told him I was staying in a cheap place in the medina," I said. "But it's not a big deal. C'mon, let's get ready to go. It'll be dark in an hour."

IN OUR ROOM the windows were open and a warm breeze blew through the curtains. A muezzin's call soared from a minaret somewhere in the town. A sense of dread was descending on me but I kept going forward, like a man walking to the gallows.

When the daylight had faded I left Marissa and went out to find a payphone. I made a trial run for later by taking the rear stairs at the end of hall, rather than going the usual route through the lobby. At the bottom of the stairs there was a metal door. It was unlocked. The courtyard was thick with shadows and I stood still a minute waiting for my eyes to adjust. The moon had waxed to a slender crescent and the stars were hot points in the darkness. Finally the shapes of the fountain and iron patio furniture became clearer. Other than the low gurgle the water made it was quiet in the court-yard; I was afraid to move, thinking my footfalls would echo through the silence, or that I would bump into something and make a racket. Feeling my way I walked under the tree and came closer to the rear wall, where the shadows deepened. I touched the cold concrete and began moving to the right. The wooden door had no knob, just an iron ring. The door squeaked open. A hallway went through the building to the alley. Faint light fell across the floor. There was a stack of plywood sheets along the wall, on top of which I discerned the shape of a hammer. I saw the back of the apartment building across the alley. A shabby elevator sat at the first floor with its door open; inside Arabic graffiti was scratched into the red paint. I could smell food cooking and hear radios and TVs, fragments of muffled voices. In the alley a rat ran past in silhouette.

When I reached the street I found a tobacco shop on the corner. A fat woman was sitting behind a counter, below a portrait of the king.

"Bon soir, madame."

"Bon soir, monsieur."

"Is there a telephone here?"

She pointed to a corner in the back. Above a rack of news-papers and magazines a payphone was mounted on the wall. Geiler answered on the third ring.

"This is Will Clark. We met in the café today?"

His voice sounded tired. "Oh yes, Clark. How are you?"

"I'm well. And you?"

"Fine, fine."

"There is something that you can help me with, after all."

His voice sweetened. "What is it?"

"You remember my associate asked you about chartering a boat?"

"Of course."

"She and two of her journalist friends want to go up the coast to Tangier. Can you arrange it?"

"It's far easier to take the train," he said.

"Yes, I know, but they're working on some sort of documentary and want to see the coastal towns from the water, in the early morning light. They need to leave tonight."

Geiler was quiet for a moment. I could tell that he didn't believe me about the documentary, but I had my own doubts about him. "It could be difficult finding someone to take them on such short notice," he said. "How much are they willing to pay?"

"Oh, I don't know. Four hundred dirhams?"

The woman behind the counter looked up at me.

"A man I know has a sailboat, nothing fancy, but it can sleep four," Geiler said. "If he is available I can arrange it for a thousand."

"That much?"

"Perhaps if you had given more notice the price would be lower."

"A thousand includes your fee?"

"A thousand even."

"All right. I think they'll agree."

"And what about you, Mister Clark? You won't be joining the young lady on this expedition?"

"No, I have an assignment in Fez, and she's looking for her own story."

Geiler and I arranged to meet at a café near the beach at nine o'clock. After I hung up with him there was one more call I needed to make.

"Madame, what is the number for the police?"

IT WAS NEARLY SEVEN-THIRTY when I returned to the hotel. The lobby was crowded and I avoided the front desk, heading straight up the stairs to the second floor. The stairwell was darker and the stars and moons shone brighter.

The room was dark except for the lamp by the bed. Marissa was lying there, fully dressed. She looked at me as I walked in.

"It's all set," I said. "We're meeting Geiler at a café near the water in an hour and a half. Where's Tammy?"

"With Nigel, in their room. You talked to the old man?"

"He knows somebody with a sailboat."

She stood and walked to me, putting her hands on my shoulders. "Will, who is this old *creep*, anyway? Maybe he's setting us up."

"I think he's all right. He just makes a little money brokering arrangements for people."

"But he's going to know that something's off," she said. "Those two idiots contradicted us."

"He's used to that. Around here everyone's hiding something."

Marissa tried to put her arms around me but I backed away. "I'm gonna take a quick shower. Go get Tammy and Nigel, and bring 'em here."

She looked hurt but I ignored it.

I was drying off when I heard them come in. I looked at my reflection in the mirror above the sink. Light from the ceiling fixture fell straight down and there were shadows under my eyes. Water was dripping down my face. I saw my father looking back at me.

Tammy and Nigel were sitting on the second bed, facing Marissa. I sat beside her.

"I talked to the man I met in the café today. He has a friend with a sailboat that sleeps four. For fifteen hundred dirhams he'll take us to Lisbon. We have to meet the old man at a café in the medina at nine."

Nigel looked at his watch. "Shite, that's an hour from now."

"What if it's another trap?" Tammy said. "I don't think I

can do this!" She bent over and put her hands on her head.

"No, sweetheart, it's going to be all right," Nigel said softly, reaching his arm around her shoulder. "It will be a huge relief to be out of this place."

"I found a way that we can leave out the back, through the courtyard," I said. "This way the hotel people won't see us leaving with our bags without even spending the night. Leave your key on the table in your room. Take the corridor to the right, and then go down the stairs. At the bottom the door opens into the courtyard. Go around the fountain to the right. There's a hallway through the coach house to the alley."

Tammy moved her hands back and forth on her legs and then rubbed her face, breathing in short bursts through her open mouth.

"Turn right in the alley, and take it to the street," I continued. "You can get a cab on the corner. Marissa and I will follow a few minutes later, but we'll go left on the street, and find a cab a block down." I opened the guidebook to a page with a map of the town. "The cab should follow the Boulevard Misr, just outside the ramparts. There's a café overlooking the beach. That's where we'll meet our man."

Everyone was quiet for a few minutes. I could hear Tammy's anxious breathing.

"I've never been so scared in my life," she said, starting to cry. "It's been almost twenty-four hours now. The cops are looking for us, for sure. Why the hell did we even come here? I should have stayed with my mother."

"We'll be in Portugal before they figure out those three goons didn't kill each other," Nigel said, rising to his feet and rubbing her shoulder. "C'mon, sweetie, let's get ready to go."

"How's your ankle, old man?"

"Aye, still a little bruised and swollen, but better now."

Everyone stood except Tammy, who was sitting on the bed looking down at the floor.

"C'mon, sweetie. We'll need to change some money downstairs."

Tammy looked at me with tears bulging in her eyes. "You'd better know what you're doing, Clark."

"Bring me your dirhams before you leave," I said. "Remember, if the cops are looking for us, they're looking for a group of four. When we get to the café we should ignore each other until I've talked to Geiler. And then Marissa will come to your table."

After they left I sat in a chair by the nightstand and stared at the light falling across the dark wood floor from the fixture above the sink. Marissa went into the bathroom and shut the door, cutting off the light. The lamp by the bed cast thin orange through the room.

Chapter Twelve

NIGEL DROPPED OFF THEIR SHARE of the money and then he and Tammy left the hotel. Marissa and I waited fifteen minutes before going. She wanted to make love again but I said no. We went down the back stairs and through the murky courtyard, trying not to knock into the furniture with our bags. She accidentally kicked the leg of an iron chair and it scraped loudly. A light shone in the room on the second level of the house behind the courtyard and I heard the voices of an Arab couple inside.

On our way through the corridor I picked up the hammer and put it in my canvas bag. We walked down the alley to the street and then stopped at the corner where the taxi had dropped us after lunch. A police car was coming toward us.

"Smile at me," I said, grinning at her.

"Oh, Darling, you're too much fun!" She threw her head back with counterfeit laughter.

The car crossed the intersection and stopped on the other side of the street from us. I acted like I didn't notice and continued looking for a taxi. A couple of student travelers were walking in our direction. Still smiling I glanced at the police car and saw vague shapes of two men in the front seat. Slowly the car began to move again.

A taxi was coming and I waved for it to stop. In its headlights I saw the faces of the young men coming toward us and recognized them from the group of backpackers we had seen talking to Tammy and Nigel at the train station that morning. We got into the car and the driver followed the boulevard along the outer perimeter of the medina. Marissa reached her hand to mine, but I did not take it. The windows were down and I stared at the base of the wall as the ocean breeze swept across us. The road went straight toward the beach and then turned left along the shore to the outskirts of the town. Before the turn the driver stopped at the café on the edge of the native quarter. I paid him and we climbed out with our bags. I smelled tobacco and hashish burning and could hear Arabic music and the sound of the waves.

The café was mostly empty, just a few men sitting around smoking. We found a table in the back, in a shadowy corner where I could see everyone coming and going. Despite having left the hotel before we did, Tammy and Nigel were not in the café. Nor was Geiler. I looked at my watch: ten minutes past nine. The waiter was a kind-looking plump man in his forties, and we ordered chicken kabobs and mineral water. It was twenty minutes later when I saw the little European gentleman enter the café. He took a table near the awning and lit a cigarette. Geiler did not look around for us. He was wearing a dark sport coat and appeared relaxed as he sat gazing at the stars over the sea.

Marissa and I were almost finished eating when Tammy and Nigel arrived.

"About damn time," Marissa said, too loudly.

I didn't look but heard the taxi stop. The doors opened and shut; the car drove away. I continued looking at Marissa and at the Arab men in the shadows behind her. Greenish light warbled from a leaded-glass lamp that was suspended on a chain from the ceiling and moved in the breeze. There was very little conversation among the men at the tables.

The atmosphere was opposite that of a bar, loud with drunken louts; here in the kif culture, the smokers were quiet and introspective. Marissa and I did not attract stares this time, as we had in the northern towns. I heard chairs scraping the floor and turned to see Tammy and Nigel sitting down at a table in the center of the café, with their bags beside them. She and Marissa were the only women there, and as usual Tammy stood out with her fair complexion and blond hair.

"Don't look at them," I said.

When we had finished eating I left Marissa at the table and crossed the café to greet Geiler.

He looked up at me and smiled. "Mister Clark, there you are." He extended his hand. I pulled back a chair and sat across from him. "My friend is waiting down the road from here in his boat," he said. "Did you bring the thousand?" Geiler knocked ash from his cigarette.

"I would like to see the vessel first."

"Of course."

"Then I'll come back to fetch my colleagues. And then I'll pay you. Okay?" I took a folded tourist pamphlet from inside my jacket and bent back the corner to show Geiler the bills inside. "Let me pay her check, and then I'll meet you outside."

I did not look at Tammy and Nigel as I walked past them to where Marissa was sitting in the back. "After I leave, wait five minutes and then go join them. Five minutes after that, come down the road together."

"I'll be watching you," Marissa said.

I stood and put a few coins on the table.

"Wait," she said. "I don't want to be here without you."

"Remember what I said. Five minutes. And then five minutes more."

I turned and walked away from her with my bags. Outside Geiler was standing with his hands in his pockets, looking at the black sea. He didn't say anything and started walking down the road.

A couple minutes later I was beside him. The wind was cool and the boom of the waves against the shore grew louder. No one else was around. To the left of the road empty earth stretched away gray and pebbly; on the right the beach was lost in darkness. I saw the lights of a few small boats on the water. Geiler led me across the road and onto the beach.

"My friend has the only sailboat in the group," he said. "We'll have to row the dinghy out there."

The boat was anchored on the dark water. Lantern light smeared the bow. I couldn't tell if anyone was aboard. The road behind us was empty.

"What have you got waiting for me here, Geiler?"

"As I said, the boat is small but reasonably clean."

I heard someone whistle. Marissa was coming up the road. I wanted to keep walking but with Geiler there I was forced to wait for her. The footing became unsteady as we started across the sand past a dark shack.

"That's his boat," Geiler said to Marissa, pointing over the black water. Yellow lights bobbed around its edges.

"And he can take us all the way to Lisbon?" she asked him.

"Lisbon? I thought you were going to Tangier."

I heard the siren and saw red and blue lights flashing across the water. A police car was coming up the road from the café. Marissa clenched my arm. And then I saw the shapes of Tammy and Nigel, black in silhouette against the white glare of the headlights, walking with their bags. The car stopped about thirty yards from us and two policemen got out. The colored lights spun over the road, the beach and the water. The men yelled to Tammy and Nigel in Arabic.

"Are those your friends?" Geiler asked with an edge in his voice, looking at me.

Tammy and Nigel stopped and turned toward the policemen, their shadows from the headlights stretching five times their body lengths over the pavement. Suddenly Nigel dropped his bag and started running down the road, limping on his twisted ankle.

"Nigel!" Tammy yelled, going after him.

The policemen stepped into the beams of the headlights and drew their pistols. They yelled in French for Nigel to stop. He was angling toward the field as he ran. One of the policemen fired into the air.

Tammy screamed again: *"NIGEL!"*

I heard more shots and saw his black outline jerk against the white background. Blood burst dark from his chest and shoulder. He staggered and fell face-down on the pavement. Tammy's screams were the most anguished sounds I had ever heard.

"Good God!" Geiler cried. Marissa gasped and squeezed my arm tighter.

Nigel was sprawled on the road. Tammy ran toward him. Another shot, fire flaring from the muzzle of the policeman's gun. Tammy's head snapped to one side. Her body spun to the ground.

I saw Geiler reaching under his sport jacket. I shoved him behind the shack and he fell to his knees on the sand. I took the hammer from my bag and held it upside down, with my fist around the steel head. Geiler tried to stand up and I whacked the wood handle against the back of his skull. He grunted and dropped back to his knees, slumping over into the sand.

Marissa and I were beside him in the pitch black. She was breathing hard. I reached under Geiler's jacket and touched his wallet, but left it there. On the other side I found a pistol in a shoulder holster.

"Son of a bitch."

I unsnapped the buckle and pulled out the gun. It looked like a European automatic, a Walther .380. Geiler was muttering. I put the gun in my bag and stuck the business card he had given me back into his pocket. A chill blew from the water and the smell of the ocean was strong. The sound of the crashing waves grew louder and the boats were clanging. I looked back at the horizon; the water was the darker hemisphere under a sky strewn electric with stars. The sand felt cool beneath my body.

Crawling forward I peered around the corner. The headlights stretched over the pavement and then faded into the darkness. I could hear the voices of the policemen talking on their radios. They were standing over Tammy and Nigel's bodies, about ten feet apart. From the roof of the car the blue and red lights flashed in a wide circle across the beach and the water and the road and the empty field on the other side. A small crowd from the café was running toward the police.

"What do we do now?" Marissa said panting, full of panic.

"I don't think the police are looking for us. Those two stood out more."

"Are they dead?"

"Nigel for sure. I don't know about Tammy."

Geiler moaned and started squirming in the sand behind me.

"Stay in the shadows," I said to Marissa. "Keep low."

I was bent over as I started running within the long shade of the shack that stretched far along the edge of the water from the low headlights of the police car. I looked back and saw Marissa dashing behind me. In the distance an ambulance sped toward the shore on the boulevard outside the medina wall.

Where the road fell back into darkness we ran across it, down into a flat expanse of gray dirt and pebbles. On the far side of the clearing there was a hill where a residential neighborhood began, in the direction of the train station.

Chapter Thirteen

I WOKE IN A SLEEPING CAR to a spectral image. Marissa's face was hidden in shadow and her little tits were bouncing as she held the luggage rack above her, groaning and thrusting herself onto me with the movement of the train. I don't remember coming. I must have fallen back asleep instantly.

The sun was hot when I woke again a few hours later. My head ached and I sat up to draw the curtain. The fabric fluttered in the wind. Marissa was sitting on the edge of the opposite berth in her panties and a white spaghetti-strap T-shirt.

"Good morning, baby," she said, smiling affectionately at me. "Three more hours until Marrakesh. We should be there by noon."

Across the red desert distant mesas slid past in the morning glare. I thought about Tammy lying on the road. She had made a big mistake trusting those guys on the train. And look where it got her. I just hoped Stacey was safe.

We passed shantytowns and mud-brick settlements, and lugubrious bergs of white apartment blocks. But mostly we saw a flat red expanse, unvarying and featureless but for plateaus along the horizon, nebulous in the dust and harsh sunlight. In the distance on a parallel road a little truck raised brown clouds behind as it sped across the basin. We passed a group of boys crouched around a well, trying to coax a donkey to pull a yoke and lift a pouch of water. The animal wasn't moving. The boys grimaced in the sun.

I thought about that night in Amsterdam two weeks earlier. As usual I was nearly broke, but the tourism board had arranged a free flight on KLM and a hotel for me after my editor said yes to two assignments I'd pitched him, one about houseboat hotels in the canals, the other about the Heineken brewery. I'd used the final credit on my Visa to buy the ticket for the train ride from Amsterdam to Madrid, and taken the last six hundred dollars out of my bank account. I had been hoping that a couple of checks would arrive before I left for the trip, but they did not. I couldn't remember how many times I'd been disappointed to open my mailbox and find it empty or stuffed only with bills. I was always waiting for checks from editors.

At first things had gone well in Amsterdam. I interviewed a woman who ran a houseboat hotel, shot some pictures of her, and spent the night. I had good notes for an article. The next day I visited the old Heineken brewery in town, now a museum, and rode the train to the modern plant on the outskirts of Amsterdam. Green glass bottles on conveyors moved on curving paths, full of beer but with the necks not yet attached, somehow without spilling. Again I had good notes and pictures. My editor at the wire service would probably pick up second rights after the stories appeared in the paper, earning me a few hundred extra dollars.

On my third night in Amsterdam I went down to the red-light district to browse the sex stores. I liked the hard-core porn magazines I found there, with their thick, glossy paper, high production quality and no ads. I bought a few. I saw the girls in the windows of the row houses by the canals and was tempted by a blonde in peach bra and panties and stiletto heels who sat on a stool with her legs crossed and the glass tilted open and said to me with a naughty grin, *"Fifty guilders, suck or fuck, yes?"* But I kept going, past more girls in storefront windows and garishly lighted businesses where men jerk themselves off in booths after putting coins into a slot to activate a shutter that slides up, revealing a naked girl dancing on the other side of the glass.

I was walking on a dark side street when from out of nowhere someone punched me in the stomach, knocking me down. My bag fell and magazines spilled across the pavement. I felt someone pull my wallet from my back pocket and looked up to see the shapes of three men standing over me. They spoke to one another in Arabic. One kicked me hard in the side and the pain joined the sock to the gut to bend me in half. I could only see their dark outlines until one of them stepped into the light of a streetlamp on the corner. I saw clearly the stranger I would later know as Fareed. I heard them laughing as they ran away.

I got to my feet and followed them, trying to stay in the shadows. My stomach and hip still hurt like hell. I followed them over footbridges that crossed the city's canals, past row houses, shops and bars on slender streets with strange electric signs, until I saw them go into a small Middle Eastern restaurant. I snuck to the edge of the window and peered inside. They were seated at a table, laughing and ordering food. Fareed was facing the window. The wallet they'd robbed from me was a decoy I used when traveling and only had about twenty dollars' worth of guilders in it. I thought about bursting in and confronting them, but instead went across the street and stood in the shadow of a tree, waiting for them to come out. People walked by and gave me uneasy looks. It was nearly two hours later, almost midnight, when Fareed and his crew finally left the restaurant. They went in separate directions but I followed him. He walked a few blocks to a row house on a back street, where he opened the door and went inside. I wrote down the address.

There was a café across the street. The next day I got up early and waited there for him to come out. I had been sitting in the café for about ninety minutes drinking tea and eating biscuits when he finally left the house. I took his picture through the window of the café. Outside I followed him on foot until he stopped at a coffee shop called The Magic Carpet Ride. He went inside.

I still wasn't sure what to do. I thought about waiting and ambushing him, giving him a beating. Maybe even killing him. But I walked back to my hotel, frustrated.

On my last night I was at a coffee shop in the Leidseplein square where I knew the guy who worked behind the counter. That afternoon I had gone to a one-hour photo shop to have my film developed. The picture of Fareed through the café window had a big reflection across one side of it, but his face was still visible. I told my friend what happened and showed him the photo. "Have you ever seen this creep before?" His eyes got bigger. He said the guy in the picture was the leader of a gang that smuggled Moroccan blond into the Netherlands. They were suspected of killing a rival in Amsterdam. In their own country they were known to rob tourists on the train.

"You know there are people who would like to see him dead," my friend said, leaning toward me across the bar.

"Yeah? Like who?"

"Never mind. I shouldn't have brought it up. He would never talk to a reporter, anyway."

"Who said I want to talk to him as a reporter?"

"Come on, Will, you don't—"

"Okay, you're right, it's for a story. But tell him I just want to talk to him on deep-background, off the record. C'mon, call him for me, man."

He took the large tip I'd left him and winked at me, and then tapped the coins on the bar before putting them in his pocket.

I waited a couple of hours for the man to arrive, vacillating between anger and wanting to forget the whole thing. Several times I almost got up and left. And then the Dutchman walked in and my friend nodded to me. He was clean-cut and conservative, maybe about thirty-five, and didn't look anything like a drug dealer. He had short brown hair and wore a polo shirt with a light jacket. He suggested we go for a walk. Outside we passed through the paved square, bordered on three sides by short gingerbread buildings bright with electric color, bars, restaurants, cafés, nightclubs. One bar had a ten-foot-high Rolling Stones logo, red black and white tongue and lips, electrified above the entrance. People milled about outside or sat at tables and chairs arranged on one side of the square. Colored lights were festooned in the trees. A crowd gathered around a man with long dark hair pulled back into a ponytail who stood in front of a coffee shop, breathing fire. He poured gasoline into his mouth from a red plastic can and then spit it out in a jet toward a lighter in his outstretched hand, which he pulled away at the instant of ignition. Hippies with tin cups played acoustic guitars. *"I'm free to do what I want, any old time."* A waifish girl swayed her hips. A tram slid through the center of the plaza, windows flashing by like stuttering frames of film. I walked with the man past inscrutable businesses with electric signs that stuck out at right angles from the façades, nearly touching across the alley. We emerged onto a path alongside a canal where neon color rode the dark surface of the water.

After half an hour of small talk and questions, the Dutchman offered me forty thousand dollars to eliminate his rival.

"You see, it's perfect," he said. "We know that he will be

going back to Morocco in a few days, and that's where you are going, too."

Forty thousand was more money than I'd ever had in my life. The thought of it sent a thrill through me. Maybe I wouldn't even return to Chicago—I could go live on the beach in Honduras or get a little place down in Lima, Peru. But I wasn't a killer. And I told the man so.

"It is not a matter of being a killer," he said in gentle tones. "It is only a matter of having the willingness and the aptitude, indeed, the temperament, to perform a particular kind of job. This is a job that needs to be done, no different than any other job, and it requires the right person to carry out the task, someone who can do the work dispassionately and yet with a commitment to quality. Quality is always very important. Given your particular personal history with the subject and the skills that you possess, you seem well suited for this task. But you must remember to leave your emotions out of it. Are you familiar with chemical engineering, Mister Clark? Chemical engineering is the application of chemistry to business problems. In my industry, assassination must sometimes be applied to business problems, in much the same way. This work is going to be done, if not by you then by someone else, so your acceptance or refusal won't matter to the subject. But the financial reward will matter a great deal to you, I should think. When you get to Madrid you will meet a contact who will give you more details. After the job is done you will return to Madrid for your payment."

He stopped and looked me in the eye. Girls were laughing as they walked past us and light from a nightclub sign fell red and orange across the Dutchman's face. "This is a good opportunity for you, and one that will not come along again," he said. "Do a good job, a thorough, professional, and high-quality job, and there will be more work for you in the future. Take the night to think about it." I had the feeling that if I said no I'd wind up at the bottom of one of the city's canals.

That night at my hotel I called home to check my answering machine. There were two messages, and both were bad news. The first was from my editor at the paper, saying that I could go ahead and finish my assignments, but they were the last he could offer me. He had just hired a full-time feature writer, a young Cuban woman that I knew, and the paper was cutting its freelance budget. Goddamn him. He had known for years that I wanted the job. I thought about the times I had ridden the subway downtown to drop off an article in a plain manila envelope with the receptionist for someone to retype into the paper's computers, seldom invited inside to meet the people I was working for. The second message was worse than the first: It was my landlord, saying that my rent check had bounced again—the second time in three months. It was almost thirty days late, again. If I didn't pay by the end of the week I would be evicted. I pictured my meager possessions tossed in the alley behind the building on Dearborn, being picked through by rats.

Sitting on the train I realized that Fareed and I had both been born to limited opportunities. Staying angry was the only way to hold back the guilt, and the fear. *"Fuck him. He had it coming."*

It was pin-needle hot when Marissa and I arrived in Marrakesh at midday. The train screeched and hissed as it shook to a stop. In the burning sun porters were carrying luggage and shouting in Arabic; a few teenage guides darted amongst the arriving passengers.

"Isn't it exciting, Darling?"

"The book says the hotel is inside the medina, just off the

main square," I said without looking at her. "Let's find a taxi."

The guides were all around us.

"Show you the medina, mister? Nice gift for your wife?"

One of the boys looked more honest than the others. "Just you," I said. "We don't need any other help."

A proud expression lifted the boy's face as he stepped forward to take Marissa's backpack. The others ran to the next car of the train.

We followed him toward a low building at the end of the gravel platform. Three uniformed men were coming toward us. Their eyes were hidden in noon shadow under the bills of their shiny hats. One of them shouted in Arabic. The men started running. Marissa gripped my arm. The train sat idling to our left; to the right were empty tracks. I could feel the weight of the pistol in the bottom of my canvas bag. The men ran past us and we turned to see them pull truncheons from their belts and begin poking the chests of the other guides, who had gathered around some middle-aged European tourists farther down the platform.

My heart was still thumping as we passed through the little station to where taxis were waiting in the hot sun. The guide led us to the first car and put our bags in the trunk. I handed him a five-dirham coin and gave the driver the address. We were outside the high salmon-colored walls surrounding the old city and rode through the rampart gate into a whirling traffic circle. Dozens of tiny cars, motorcycles and scooters were buzzing and spraying diesel exhaust. Donkeys and horses pulled wooden carts through the chaos. We shot onto a side street, past men in djellabas and women in veils. The buildings in the medina were all one or two stories high, and the same red-earth color. An old woman with a cane walked along bent in half, her chest parallel to the ground.

The driver stopped in front of the hotel. A man was standing in the doorway, wearing a gold turban and a silky white robe with gold piping. I paid the driver and we stepped into the burning dry sun. I could smell meat grilling and hear music. The doors to the modest hotel were propped open. There was no air conditioning in the lobby but the dark space was cool. The two-story hotel had six rooms on each floor, bordering a rectangular courtyard. There were skylights over the courtyard and the sun drove down in heavy beams, illuminating the red clay walls. A boy took us up a stairway to the second floor, where a balcony led to the rooms. The door was open and our room smelled of disinfectant. A girl of twelve with a cloth around her head walked out carrying a mop and bucket. She looked at me with green eyes that were shockingly beautiful and then lowered them as she passed. She was one of those girls with startling eyes who end up being quiet and reserved because of all the attention they receive. Everyone wants to possess her beauty, an urgent desire that competes with a fear of rejection that increases the desire to possess her even more, spinning in a maddening circle.

The room's only window faced the courtyard. I tipped the boy and Marissa went into the bathroom for a shower. I pulled a chair onto the walkway outside our door and watched an old woman working below. She looked like a Sudanese slave, with a drab cloth around her head and a gray apron. With an expression weary but beneficent she held up a heavy rug and began beating it with a broom handle. Dust huffed into the air, drifting through the diffused areas of light and bursting into the bright beams.

OUTSIDE THE MARRAKESH AFTERNOON BLAZED dry heat in rust colored dust. We walked through crooked alleys under phallic archways, past studded, brown-metal doors in the walls surrounded by zigzag patterns of yellow and blue tile. From restaurants the size of closets men grilled kabobs for people walking by in the street. The smoky aroma of the meat made my stomach snarl. I looked around for Stacey, hoping and dreading to see her.

From behind a stack of wooden crates a deformed beggar suddenly appeared. His legs were twisted around, with his feet facing backward. He dragged himself toward us on a cane bracing his forearm, smiling and holding out a cup with his other hand.

"Oh, Lord!" Marissa said as she squeezed my elbow and began walking faster. "How did the poor man end up like that?"

"Polio, probably."

We followed the bending street to where it met the djemaa el fna, the "assembly of the dead." Cafés surrounded the sprawling square, where hundreds of vendors and performers sang out for attention. Drumming and the smell of grilling meat filled the air. Water sellers in red robes and conical red hats roamed the crowd, yellow tassels swinging from the wide brims. The men had goatskin bags full of drinking water slung across their backs, the straps festooned with brass cups. People were gathered around a turbaned man who sat cross-legged on a rug, playing a clarinet as a black cobra rose from a basket in front of him. Veiled women sat selling produce as their children played nearby. Carts full of oranges gleamed in the sun. Arabic voices and music filled the square, hypnotic melodies and drums. Natives outnumbered tourists ten-to-one, and only the vendors noticed us as we wandered among the crowd. Through the shifting vistas I glimpsed a few European tourists in the background. More than once my heart jumped when I saw long blond hair. But it wasn't her.

At the edges of the square in the tunnels of the souks,

sunlight splintered through thatch roofs over rows of shop stalls, cutting down in sharp blades through the drifting dust, senses bombarded by color, light, voices, music, scents of perfume and spice and leather and cedar wood. In one stall a man was surrounded by trays of nuts that slanted up like the side of a roof, with only his head and shoulders visible through a square hole in the center. He smiled at us as we passed.

Another man stepped into our path and grabbed my sleeve. "Excuse me, sir; did you drop your money?" I shook my head and kept walking.

Men crowded the narrow aisles in the souks, robed turbaned figures gathered at intersections where one path would split into several others, in shadows or beams of shifting dust. Others crouched in smoky stalls pounding red-hot metal into tea kettles and frying pans to be offered for sale in nearby booths. The hammers clanged in a bitter smoking din.

WE ATE LUNCH AT A ROOFTOP CAFÉ overlooking the square. Marissa talked as though the events of the previous two days had never happened, rambling selfishly about her job at the frame store, her divorced parents, her sister in Paris. But she didn't mention Tammy.

"I think I can find a pilot," I said. "A small plane to fly us out of the country, into Algeria. Then we can work our way north and get a boat to Italy."

My reference to the subject we had been avoiding seemed to catch her unawares. Marissa's face darkened. "You know what's happening in that country. We can't go there."

"I think it's much more dangerous for the Algerians than it would be for us."

She looked out over the square and the lowering sunlight

shone on her eyes. "C'mon, Will. Where are you gonna find a pilot?"

"I have an idea."

THAT EVENING AT THE HOTEL Marissa sat in a chair reading while I lay on the bed and studied the guidebook. It was quiet. Even with the window to the courtyard open and the doors of many of the other rooms ajar and the European tourists occasionally visible within them, all I could hear was the soft wobble of the pages that Marissa turned in her book every few minutes. I fell asleep.

When I woke she was sleeping next to me on the bed. She had turned off the lamp and the room was dark except for a wan glow through the curtains. It was nearly eight o'clock and my stomach was rumbling again.

"I'm going to find something more to eat," I said.

She opened her eyes and sat up in the bed. "I'll go with you."

Outside we walked through crooked alleys in the dark. At the djemma el fna sounds and aromas clamored in the cool night. The air was filled with the music of drumming, bright finger symbols and buzzing clarinets; people yelling and laughing in voices at once guttural and melodic; smells of meat grilling and diesel exhaust, cigarette smoke and citrus fruits, livestock and perfume. The awnings over the food carts had strings of lights around the edges and they dimmed blurred and glowed brighter as smoke floated past from the grills. Vendors crouched over wares spread on rugs, orange lanterns throwing strange shadows across their faces. Marissa held my arm as we walked through the crowd of sellers and storytellers and acrobats and musicians. Trance repetitions nagged from Moroccan clarinets. The smell of kabobs grilling in the cool air of the desert night made me hungrier than I had ever felt. A swarthy man with a green cap and a beak nose was cooking skewers of lamb and chicken over a charcoal fire. We ordered half a dozen kabobs of the crunchy, juicy lamb and a plate of French fries, and ate standing at the counter. Marissa seemed edgier now, her eyes always moving, looking around at the faces. We barely spoke.

We finished our food and continued walking through the square. A man in a brown djellaba and skullcap stood over a wooden cart selling vials of homemade perfume. A lantern cast amber light over one half of his lined face; the other side was black in shadow. Marissa stopped to look at the perfumes, holding the vials close to her nose. In the air were evanescent wisps of vanilla, citrus and flowers, and then a blast of cigarette smoke and the unmistakable scent of hashish burning—sharp, sweet and spicy. In a café men were sitting under an awning almost completely obscured in darkness; only the outlines of their heads were visible in silhouette against a dull glow from inside.

WHEN WE REACHED THE HOTEL I stopped. "Go up to the room and wait for me. I'm heading back to the square."

She looked at me with suspicious alarm. "What are you talking about?"

"I think I know where I can find a connection for a pilot. I can get it done faster if I'm alone. Just wait for me here."

Her brown eyes brimmed with anger and doubt. The line between them deepened. "What are you doing, Will?"

"You know how they are about women here. Let me go talk to some people."

Marissa searched my eyes and then I saw her guard fall. "All right," she said. "But come upstairs with me first."

The courtyard was dark. There was only a weak light through the curtains of a couple rooms on the second floor.

Our footfalls echoed as we climbed the unlit stairs. In the room I snapped on the lamp by the bed.

"Keep the door locked, but have your bags packed in case we have to leave fast."

She looked at me and bit her lower lip.

"We should leave before dawn," I said, not looking at her.

"You're not coming back, are you?"

"What?"

"Cut the bullshit, Clark. You're planning to leave me here, aren't you?"

"No."

"Yes, you are. I can feel it. And don't give me that crap about flying out of here to Algeria, because I don't buy it."

"You're crazy."

"I am not your whore!"

"No, just Alain's."

She looked at me and narrowed her eyes, breathing hard through her nose. "I could be pregnant. Have you thought about that?"

My stomach felt sick. "What?"

"You came inside me, remember?"

I took the gun from my bag, checked the clip, saw it was full, and then pushed the .380 down under my belt, covering up the handle with my jacket.

"Wait for me here," I said. "I'll be back."

"Your bags stay here."

"You don't control me."

"And you're not leaving me here, you son of a bitch!"

She swung at me and I grabbed her fist with my left hand, swatting her across the face with the back of my right. Marissa fell against the edge of the bed and sat hard on the floor. In the dim light I saw blood running down from the corner of her mouth.

"You tried to make it seem like it was all Tammy's decision, but it wasn't by chance that we got off the train with those creeps," she said, blood slurring her words and tears falling from her eyes. "I saw the photos in your bag. I know you went there to kill them!"

Chapter Fourteen

I LEFT THE HOTEL and stood outside for a moment before walking down the dark path toward the lights and drumming. In the other direction a man standing against a wall lit a cigarette and for an instant I saw his face in the glow of the fire. He seemed to be looking at me. I started toward the square, seeing no one ahead of me in the crooked alley, only the vague outlines of crowds moving among the clamor. There was a tiny restaurant in the wall and I stopped to look at a man cooking inside. I glanced behind me and saw the shape of the man with the cigarette following in the shadows. I continued toward the square, listening over my shoulder for him. When I reached the djemma el fna I merged into the throng, bending down a couple of times pretending to look at some knickknack and then turning in another direction as I stood.

Through the mosaic of faces and lights and the cacophony of voices and music I heard English being spoken and laughter and I saw standing near a café a group of young travelers that included a girl with long blond hair. I started toward them but a vendor was suddenly in my way, importuning me in Arabic to buy some carved trinket. I stepped around him but the group of travelers had moved behind some high carts out of my view. I turned back and didn't see the man. Drums were beating and clarinets played shrill halftone scales and nearby a man juggled fire. I heard British and Australian accents and maybe German and again saw light landing on a flow of long blond hair down a girl's back but as I progressed closer another group blocked my view of the first. I looked through the crowds for her. And then I saw the man again. I ducked behind the awning of a food counter and slipped into a café on the perimeter of the square. Men were sitting on cushions on platforms smoking cigarettes and hashish and drinking tea. There were seats along the sides that looked in toward the center and a stairway that led to a gallery on the second floor. I sat next to a young man with a moustache who immediately offered me his cigarette and I accepted with a nod of thanks, drawing the tobacco and hashish smoke into my lungs. He seemed happy to have me beside him and not interested in hustle or chitchat and we sat there staring into the center and smoking until the long cigarette had burned down. The pistol was in my belt and I pulled down the bottom of my jacket to cover it. I was thirsty and when the waiter came I ordered tea for myself and the man. From where I sat I could see the entrance to the café and people moving by outside and I looked for blond heads that might be Stacey and for the man who may or may not have been following me, trying to manage the alternating buffets of hope and threat that the thoughts sent through my mind.

When we had drunk a couple small cups of tea I thanked the man who shared his smoke with me and stepped back outside, feeling the hashish in my head. Looking around I couldn't see the tourists anymore. I made a couple of passes through the square and then started down a dim alley toward the hotel. A couple of teenagers called out to me in Arabic and I kept on walking, ignoring them. The hashish had brought on a delayed effect and suddenly I felt it much stronger than I had earlier. When I came to the intersection of a couple of dark paths I stood still for a moment, not sure which one to take. In the silence I heard footsteps coming behind me. I looked over my shoulder and saw the dark shape of a man. I turned down the alley to the right where there were no shops. There was an alcove in the wall that led to the door of a house and I turned into it and peered back through the darkness. I listened for the man but heard only my heartbeat. I put my hand on the butt of the gun. The square was several blocks away and where I stood it was dead silent except for the sound of drumming in the distance. I wouldn't dare use the gun here. I wished I still had my switchblade. I heard a sound. It required an enormous effort to stand there and wait. Without thinking I pulled the Walther from my belt and turned into the alley. "*Come out, you dirty fuck!*" My heart was jumping in my chest, making me dizzy. The drums were pounding. I swallowed hard but couldn't see anyone. I kept the gun at my side and started walking back in the direction from which I'd come. There were other alcoves in the walls, pitch black, and I spoke aloud to the empty silence: "*I'm here, you prick. Come and get me.*" I spun all the way around and saw no one, and then I was at the intersection of another path, one that had some lights down its length, and suddenly there was an old man shuffling along in a djellaba and a white beard. I shoved the gun back under my belt but thought he might have seen it. A little farther down the block there was a little store; light fell from the entrance across the pavement and I stood there in its path, feeling somehow safer in the electric illumination and the long shadow from it that trailed across the ground and up the side of the adjacent wall. My heartbeat slowed and I began to wonder if there had ever been a man following me at all. But just then, in the light from another shop door, I saw him again, the one whose face had briefly appeared in the orange glow of the cigarette lighter in the street outside the hotel. I heard the drums and turned and walked fast down the alley. As the path neared the square it widened slightly and there was a stack of crates on the right; I hid behind them and waited for the man to come. I saw somebody through the gaps in the crates. He stepped forward. I swung around and punched him in the face. He stumbled back into the light, holding his jaw and looking at me with shock and anger. It wasn't the same man. Dread dropped down through me.

"Pardon, monsieur, désolé."

The man started yelling at me in Arabic and I ran down the alley away from him. The drug was strong in my head and I became confused about where the hotel was. I could hear the drums and the sounds of the square but then I would turn into another street and they would fade away. Finally I saw the entrance to the hotel at the end of a long dark street like a trench between the high walls. I started toward it when I heard the voice: *"Hey, asshole."*

I turned and saw him there in the murky light. "What do you want?"

"You like playing with knives?"

The blade glinted as he whipped it toward my neck. I leaped back and tripped over the uneven pavement, falling onto my side as he rushed toward me. There was no time to grab the gun. My right foot went up and I shoved my heel into his groin as the blade of the knife swiped before me again. He doubled over and I seized his right arm with both of my hands, twisting him down onto the ground at my left. I heard the knife skitter across the pavement. I was on top of him now and started punching him in the face and head, hearing it whack the cement after every blow. The man was grunting and grinding his teeth and swearing at me. Somewhere a dog started barking and I looked up and down the street for other people. Shadows moved toward me in the darkness. I jumped up and dragged the man backwards by his wrists into an alcove behind a pile of sand where workers had been digging during the day. I sat on his chest and pressed the muzzle of the gun against his forehead, looking at him and glancing to the side, listening for someone to pass. He was breathing hard and squirming beneath me. I heard the rattle and scrape of someone picking the knife off the street and I held my left palm over the man's mouth. Voices died down the alleyway.

"Who are you, and what do you want?"

It seemed like he might cry. "You lousy American bastard, you killed my brother!"

"Who are you talking about? Who was your brother?"

"My brother was Adir Yassan. You cut his neck open, you coldhearted son of a dog."

My heart was pounding and I felt my guts dropping inside me. "You're wrong. I don't even know your brother."

"You are a lying devil. I saw you with him in our village. You beat up our friend before you left on the train, and the next morning our mother found Adir and our cousin and his friend dead, butchered like lambs. You did that to my brother, to my mother's son!"

I was feeling dizzy as I tried to keep the muzzle of the .380 from sliding off his forehead.

"I didn't want to do it. He had my friend, a woman, by the throat and was threatening to kill her. I pleaded with him to let her go. But he wouldn't. Do you understand me, he wouldn't let her go!"

"So you slaughtered him and my cousin." He let out a desperate cry. "I'm going to kill you, you motherfucking pig!"

"What did you think was going to happen to them, when they were robbing travelers on the train, selling drugs, extorting people, huh? He wrote his own fate."

"You better kill me now, you motherless devil. Because as soon as I break free I'm going to tear your rotten heart out."

I looked over the pile of sand and up and down the alley, seeing no one. I couldn't pull the trigger here, couldn't leave him for someone to find. I jumped back and stood, pointing the gun at his chest.

"Get up."

"Fuck you."

I kicked him in the hip, just as Fareed had done to me in Amsterdam. In anger he rose on his forearms and then was standing in front of me.

"Now start walking away from the square, toward the medina wall. I'll be right behind you. If you try to run I'll shoot you in the kidneys."

I followed him through a gate in the high wall and into a flat open field. There was a length of twine on the ground and I picked it up. No one else was around. The moon was a curved white sliver and stars emerged from the dark beyond the lights of the town. A chill slid on the wind.

PART III

Chapter Fifteen

THE MORNING WAS SUNNY and clear. I sat in the back seat of a plain Mercedes sedan as the taxi driver headed south through the desert, red hills dotted with green shrubs and patches of long, lime-green grass. Rock formations knifed the sky. I leaned against the passenger-side door with my legs stretched across both seats. The windows were down and breeze filled the car. Sunlight shone on the two-lane road ahead and there were no other vehicles in sight.

We had been driving for about forty-five minutes when the driver looked at me and smiled, rubbing his belly. There was a café on the roadside and he pulled over. At a small round table we ordered morning tea with croissants and jam. We were the only paying customers in the café. An old beggar with a white beard, dressed in a gray turban and robe, sat on the floor with his knees up, leaning against a powder-blue wall. He sat on the concrete floor a couple of feet from the relative comfort of a long rug patterned in shades of blue and gold. The old man grimaced and looked out at the hills.

In the sunlight I could see the details of the driver's face as he sat across the little table from me, quietly eating his breakfast. He was probably forty years old and underneath a stubbly beard his cheeks were round and pink. The pupils in his light-brown eyes were small and sharp, and his hair parted cleanly along the left side of his head and swept up in waves.

"What is your name?"

"Mohammed."

The tea had cooled enough for me to bring the glass to my lips. "I want you to drive me over the mountains, to Zagora. But I don't want to get there until tonight, so the light will be right for taking pictures. We need to find some place to stop for a few hours. I'll pay you for your time."

He looked at me and nodded in agreement.

A thin boy of about thirteen came into the café carrying a homemade violin that consisted of a stick nailed to a rusty metal box. It had one string. The bow was a stick with a wire tied between the ends. The boy's expression matched the sound as he began playing a lachrymose melody and singing in a whining voice. His eyes were full of emotion. When he came to our table I gave him a five-dirham coin and he kissed my hand.

Mohammed and I finished our breakfast. I paid the waiter and also gave the old beggar a few dirhams. He took the money and moved his lips but did not speak and continued looking at the hills.

Back in the taxi we resumed up the empty two-lane blacktop. To the left down a long dirt trail mud huts were built against a brown hillside. Mohammed looked at me in the rearview mirror and pointed toward the village, raising his eyebrows.

"No. Someplace more secluded."

By now it was eight-thirty in the morning and a few other vehicles had passed us going the other way, a small car, a truck, a bus. A white line divided the road and the strip of pavement rolled out ahead of us and then bent behind trees and red hills dusted with green scrub. The hills repeated in nebulous layers into the distance.

I was falling asleep but suddenly sat up as Mohammed turned the taxi and started up a dirt path. It climbed and curved around a stand of conifers to a clearing at the top where we bumped along over a rocky surface, eventually passing more trees and shrubs before arriving at a small dwelling made of red mud. In front of the house there was an awning held up by four poles, above a rug spread on the ground.

Mohammed parked the car under a tree and we got out. There was a fresh breeze. Morning shadows were still long and we stood in the dappled shade. Mohammed called out in Moghrebi and a man emerged from the little house. He was tall and thin and wore khaki trousers with sandals, a reddish-brown robe and white turban. The man smiled and waved when he saw Mohammed, but his expression tightened as he noticed me. The two friends approached one another and embraced. Mohammed turned and gestured toward me, speaking to the other in his language. The tall man bowed slightly but did not smile.

He took us inside for a tour of his home. We walked into a courtyard with a dirt floor where sunlight angled in through a rectangular hole in the ceiling. At the rear of the courtyard an opening in the wall led to another room; a woman and a young girl peered around the corner at us, and then quickly withdrew. We followed the man up a stairway to a space with a low ceiling, where we crouched on the mud-brick floor and looked through an opening in the wall toward where the taxi sat beneath the trees.

Back outside we reclined on cushions under the awning while the man boiled water for tea on a charcoal brazier. His name was Abdelouahaid. We relaxed and he started to become friendlier.

"You dress like all the Americans," he said in French, laughing and pointing at my blue jeans and cotton shirt.

"Do you see many Americans around here?" I asked him.

"Not here, in Marrakesh. My wives sell our vegetables there. Sometimes I go and sit in the cafés."

"I enjoy the cafés myself."

"Do the men sit in cafés in America?"

"Not so much. All people in America do is work."

"Even the men?"

"Yes, everyone. They work every minute, and then they buy more than they can afford, so they go deeply into debt. They don't know how to live."

"This is something I do not understand," Abdelouahaid said, frowning. "If the people are free, why don't they enjoy life more?"

"They think they're free, but they're really not. Maybe that's why I'm here."

The water began to boil, hisses and pings against the tin and hot sloshing as the kettle rocked back and forth. It began screeching and steam shot into the air. Abdelouahaid stepped quickly to take the kettle off the fire. After he had brewed the tea we sat and sipped our drinks, snacking on dates and not saying much. Mohammed was quiet but looked contented. Later the women prepared a vegetable couscous for us. I thanked Abdelouahaid for his hospitality.

After the early lunch I fell asleep on the cushions beneath the awning that moved in the breeze, and it was nearly two o'clock when I woke. At first I did not see Mohammed or Abdelouahaid. I sat up with a start and reached inside my canvas bag to touch the metal of the gun. And then I saw the taxi was still there by the trees. A minute later the two men were walking out of the mud house. I looked at my watch.

"Mohammed," I called to him. "It's time to go."

They walked over to me. I shook Abdelouahaid's hand.

"For your trouble," I said, giving him a one-hundred-dirham note.

He nodded and accepted the money. "You will arrive safely in the desert tonight," he said, smiling. "Incha'Allah."

Chapter Sixteen

WE WERE BACK ON THE ROAD for thirty minutes when I saw the bus parked next to the café, right on schedule. Tourists were climbing down from the door. My heart leapt as the sun reflected off her long blond hair. It was Stacey.

"Mohammed, pull over!"

He swung the taxi off the road and the tires ground through the gravel. As soon as the car stopped I had the door open and was jumping out. More tourists were leaving the bus and a dozen stood between me and Stacey. Most of them were young, probably students or recent graduates from Europe and Australia. I saw a few older people in the group.

I came up behind her and looked at her hair. Its color and texture, and the perfect shape of her head, hit me like a drug.

"Don't I know you from somewhere?"

She turned and looked at me with her blue eyes. They lit up and she smiled. "Oh, my God, Will!" Stacey put her arms behind my neck and mine went around her waist. "This is unbelievable!"

"I had a feeling I might run into you on this road. It's the only one from Marrakesh to the desert."

A young man with brown hair parted in the middle was suddenly standing next to her, looking at me with a sour expression. "Who is this?" he asked in a German accent.

"Frank, this is my friend, Will Clark."

We looked at each other with instant mutual loathing.

"How are you," I said flatly, reaching to shake his hand.

"Frank and I met on the bus," Stacey said.

"Like you and I met in Madrid?"

Frank looked at me poisonously and then turned to her. "I will go and find a table for us, Stacey."

"Don't tell me you're jealous?"

"Should I be?"

"C'mon, he's just a friendly guy." She looked around. "Where's Marissa?"

"She went to Casablanca."

Stacey's face glowed. "Really? With your other friends, the American girl and the Englishman?"

I saw Frank turn to look back at me. "Irishman, actually," I said. "No, we split off from them in Rabat. They wanted to do their own thing, I guess. Hey, speaking of Rabat, what happened to you there?"

She made a face and then looked away. "You were busy with Marissa."

The passengers had sat down and were ordering late lunches from the only waiter in the café. Hooves and other sheep and goat parts were scattered on the dusty ground behind it.

Stacey looked at me dubiously. "So, you just coincidentally happened by? Out here, in the middle of nowhere?"

"You're not happy to see me?"

"Yeah, but ..."

"Actually, I'm surprised you've come this far already," I said. "Were you trying to catch up with me?"

She ignored my question. "You've been traveling alone?"

"Yeah."

"Where are you going?"

I squinted toward the road. *Don't tell her*, I thought. But then I said it anyway: "Over the mountains, down into the Sahara. There are some big dunes past Zagora. There's an old Kasbah nearby that they've turned into a hotel. I figure I'll stay there for a few nights, and then decide where to go next."

Her face relaxed. "I think the bus is going there, too. But not until tomorrow. Tonight we're staying in some village in the hills."

I couldn't stand the idea of Stacey spending the night with Frank.

She looked at Mohammed standing next to his car by the side of the café. "You've got that whole taxi to yourself?"

I could tell that she was hoping I would ask her to come with me, but now that I had found her, guilt spread through my guts as I realized what a bad idea it was. But my desire for her was overwhelming. And I wanted to take her away from that damned arrogant German.

"Why don't you come with me?"

"But I've already paid for my bus ticket."

I knew she didn't mean what she was saying. "That's all right. I'll pay for the car. And you'll be more comfortable than on the bus."

She gave me another of her searching, uncertain looks, incredulous, intrigued and amused. "Are you sure you want me to come with you?"

"Of course. Why wouldn't I be?" Dread dripped through my insides. "But how do I know you won't pull another disappearing act on me?" I forced a smile. "I can't have you running off into the desert by yourself."

She laughed. "Okay, Daddy, I'll try to be good. But I want to eat something first."

I leaned close to kiss her but she ducked away from me, winking and smiling before turning to walk to a table. Mohammed stayed by the car and Stacey and I wound up sitting with Frank. The café was serving mutton tagine and freshly baked pita bread. I asked for a tall bottle of mineral water, con gas.

"How long have you been in Morocco, Will?" Frank asked in his crunching German accent.

"Just a few days."

"Your first time in the country?"

"Yes."

"Not for me. Two summers ago I was in the Canary Islands and then came here to Agadir and Essaouira."

"Frank is in graduate school in Munich," Stacey said. "International business."

He looked at me imperiously. "What is your line of work, Will?" Stacey lowered her eyes.

"I write newspaper articles."

"Really? For what newspapers?"

"The Chicago Today, and others. Some magazines, too."

"Have you found any good stories in Morocco?" he asked me.

"Just one."

I looked at Stacey. She was wearing her black jacket and turquoise top and skin showed below her neck, smooth and golden. Her blond hair was thick and glossy, eyes young and unspoiled. I wanted to possess her beauty, to envelop myself around it. Her eyes, skin, lips, breasts and hair made her painfully attractive for me. I realized that I was in love with her.

"I probably will write a story about Marrakesh, maybe on the assembly of the dead," I said, talking to Frank but still looking at her. "And maybe a piece about the trip over the mountains. Stacey, you've got a camera, don't you?"

"Yes, and it's a good one, too."

"Well then, why don't you ditch this tour bus and ride with me in the taxi? We can stop along the way for you to take pictures. You'll get fifty bucks for each one they use.

More if the wire picks up the story."

"That would make no sense," Frank protested. "You have already paid for your bus ticket."

"It makes perfect sense," I said. "She'll earn more selling the pictures than what she paid for the ticket."

"How does she know you really work for any newspaper? Stacey, why don't you ask him to show you some credentials?"

She looked at me resignedly. "Well, how about it, Will?"

"Sure, in my bag, in the car. I'll get them now. Excuse me."

Mohammed was standing by the taxi, talking with a Moroccan man who had come walking up the road. In the back seat I dug into my bag for the letters. My fingertips touched the gun. A voice in my head told me to leave, to get in the car with Mohammed and drive away. I knew it would be a mistake to ignore the voice. But I walked back to the table anyway.

"Here you go," I said, handing a folded sheet of paper to Stacey.

"To whom it may concern," she began, reading the letter. "Freelance writer William Clark is doing one or more stories on Morocco for the Chicago Today's Travel section. Although Today policy requires that our writers pay for all their travel expenses—"

"The cheap bastards," I said.

Frank sneered. Stacey giggled. "—we would appreciate it," she continued, "if you could extend to him any non-monetary assistance in regard to his coverage of these stories."

"Does that meet your standards, Frank?" He looked at me with hate in his eyes.

"You're done eating," I said to Stacey. "Ready to get out of here?"

She slapped her thighs and stood up. "Let's go."

"I hope you know what you are doing," Frank said.

"I'm a big girl," she told him. "We'll see you again in a couple of days." She leaned over to hug him goodbye.

Chapter Seventeen

MOHAMMED PUT HER BAG into the trunk of the taxi and Stacey and I got into the back seat. We were sitting close, our arms and legs touching. She was warm against me, radiating romantic sexual energy. Love euphoria welled in my chest. I could feel the heat of my own blood and the adrenalin from knowing that we were about to drive over the mountains. The air was clean.

"I'm happy to see you," I said, kissing her. Stacey kissed me back but then gently pushed away, looking at Mohammed in his rearview mirror. His eyes were fixed straight ahead as he started the engine and shifted the car into gear, pulling the sedan off the gravel shoulder and onto the two-lane blacktop. The vista spread out in front of us: The land dropped and there were evergreen shrubs just below the road, nearly the size of trees. In the valley patches of green spread across the dark red earth.

"This scenery is unbelievable," she said.

"Wait 'til you see what's coming."

"What do you mean?"

"You know, the Atlas."

"I thought these were the Atlas," she said, sweeping her arm over the view.

"No, this is just the Anti-Atlas, the foothills. The real

mountains are much higher and rockier."

"And the road we're taking goes over them?"

"Yeah."

For the first time I saw vulnerability in her. Stacey squeezed my leg and I put my arm around her shoulder, holding her waist with my other.

"Have you seen the Atlas before?"

"No, but I've read about them."

The car swerved. Stacey yelled, "Whoa!" Mohammed was dodging potholes. A small truck sped past going the other way, the driver cursing and sounding his horn.

Mohammed turned to me and shrugged, a smile across his fleshy, unshaven cheeks. He had a calm and charming way about him.

"The road is full of potholes," I said.

"More like ditches."

"Which reminds me: Why do you keep ditching me? First in Madrid and then in Rabat."

She looked out the window at the valley below the road. The slopes were eroded into massive brown furrows that were filling with shadow in the late-afternoon sunlight, and a row of mountain ridges led to the horizon. The vegetation had thinned and the land was dry.

"You were sharing a hotel room with another girl," Stacey said. "I'm not a fool."

"I never thought you were a fool. I only shared a room with her because it was the only one available in the hotel. And there were two beds."

The windows of the taxi were open and her hair stirred in the breeze.

"Did anything happen?"

"No, of course not," I lied. "She acts like she can't stand me, and I feel the same way about her."

Stacey rolled her eyes. "When a girl acts like she can't

stand a guy, it's because she secretly desires him. She resents his power over her."

I laughed. "Well, I really can't stand Marissa. There's no secret about that."

"But why did you split off from your other friends?"

Mohammed glanced at me in the rearview mirror.

"Something was going on with Tammy and Nigel. They must have been fighting on the train from Lisbon before we met them. She was in a bad mood then, and seemed to stay that way. Marissa was a self-righteous pain in the ass, as always. Nigel wanted to be the leader of the group, always trying to boss me around. I was glad when they decided to go off on their own."

"I would never put up with anyone telling me what to do," Stacey said, turning again to look out the window. Terraced levels of lime-green farming plots descended the hillsides, the color bright in the sun and moving in the wind. The two-lane highway was inclining. Looking ahead I caught my first sight of the massive peaks of the High Atlas, impossibly high in the sky, black and sharp and broken, frosted with ice and snow. "Christ, look at that."

Stacey leaned forward for a better view. "Holy shit! We're going way up there?"

"Not all the way to the top. But pretty high."

She looked at the towering jagged rock and chewed the end of her finger, shifting in her seat. We rode along in silence for a few minutes and then she composed herself.

"So, after your other friends split off from you in Rabat, you went to Marrakesh with Marissa?"

"Yes, unfortunately. I was hoping she would go with them, but she didn't. It seemed like there was starting to be some tension between Marissa and Tammy, too."

Stacey brushed her hair back from her eyes with her fingertips. "You said she went to Casablanca by herself?"

"She flew up there."

"Why?"

"We'd had enough of each other. We couldn't agree on anything. Finally I wanted to go to the desert, and she wanted to see Casablanca. I was relieved to be rid of her."

I looked at the empty highway ahead of us. Scrubby gray mountainside rose on our right and dropped away on our left. The road had been gradually inclining and the valleys deepened and spread over immense distances. Looking down we could see a ruined mountain on the valley floor. Probably once fertile with soil and trees, it might later have passed epochs under the sea but now the erstwhile mountain was a stack of round plates of rock rising in progressively smaller concentric circles, like an inverted funnel, jet black.

"My God, Will. What is this place?"

The car swung to the right as Mohammed took a switchback turn. There were no guardrails and the tires rolled within inches of the edge through loose gravel and dirt.

"Tell him to slow down!"

Mohammed smiled at me in the rearview mirror. The car swung around again, this time to the left, as we completed another hairpin. We were taking another hard right when we heard a horn blaring. A bus was coming straight at us. The road was too narrow. Stacey squeezed my leg.

"It's all right," I said. "He knows what to do."

Mohammed and the bus driver both stopped, and then Mohammed pulled to the right, bringing the taxi nearly against the wall of the mountain. The bus driver shifted and the gears ground noisily as the gray rattletrap rolled down the decline, taking the sharp turn slowly and passing us. I saw faces in the windows, turbaned Berbers and Arabs, and an inevitable blond tourist or two. Mohammed continued up the mountainside and finally we came through the last in the series of switchback turns, at least for a while, as a straightaway inclined ahead of us alongside the mountain.

"I shouldn't have sat on this side," Stacey said, staring anxiously at the drop.

"Look at me."

Her eyes beguiled with contradictions, by turns sexy and powerful, then vulnerable and naïve.

"I want to know more about you," she said.

My arm was around her shoulder. "I'll tell you whatever you want to know."

"Do you have brothers and sisters?"

"None."

"What does your father do?"

"He was a policeman. But he was killed. Shot in the line of duty."

"Oh... I'm so sorry, Will."

We could no longer see the peaks of the Atlas, just the grayish brown mountainside on our right, and the valley with its strange rock shapes to the left. My ears popped as the road went higher.

"Are you close to your mother?" Stacey asked me.

"Not really." I wanted to change the subject. "What about you? Tell me about your family."

Stacey sighed and rolled her eyes. "Oh, you know, Dysfunction Central."

We were climbing and turning through hairpins again. Stacey and I fell against each other as the car swung right and left.

"My parents got divorced when I was nine," she said. "And then they both remarried with jerks."

"What does your father do?"

"He's the general manager of a TV station, an ABC affiliate. He and his golf buddies also do real estate deals. They buy and develop these tacky strip malls, and then sell them.

They make a ton of money. But my father thinks he's a king. He treated my mother like shit. Not that she's any prize, either."

"Brothers and sisters?"

Stacey looked out the window. We were much higher now and the valley fell farther. Long gray lines streaked the desert floor past the desiccated mountains.

"Just my little brother, Eddie. He's severely autistic. He'll never be able to live on his own."

"That must be hard for your family."

"My parents couldn't deal with it. He's nineteen now and they've got him living in a group home. *Oh, shit, Will!*"

We had come through a turn and now the road stretched ahead of us in a long straightaway, narrow and without guardrails, the mountain continuing its climb on the right and plunging deep into shadows on the left. A mile ahead the slender ledge turned at a ninety-degree angle to the left, granting perspective to see it strung like a ribbon across the vast belly of gray rock, thousands of feet above the valley.

"Will, tell him to stop!"

"It's all right," I said, holding her hand. "He's going slow, and there aren't any other cars around."

She bent over, her head between the two front seats, breathing hard. "No. Please. Will. Tell him to stop."

Mohammed rolled the taxi close to the wall of the mountain and brought it to a stop. A ten-foot width of road lay between the car and the precipice.

"I can't get out on this side," she said, nearly hyperventilating.

I opened the door and stepped into the tight space between the car and the wall, taking a couple of steps backward. Stacey hurried out and crouched there in the shadows.

"Getting out of the car here is a bad idea," I said.

"The bad idea was coming here in the first place!" she

yelled, looking at the ground by her feet. "I'm scared shitless of heights."

I looked ahead of the car. The road was in the shadows, but the lowering sun still shone over the perpendicular face to the left. The gray precipice was streaked with long vertical furrows that were beginning to fill with darkness.

"We've only got an hour of daylight left," I said, kneeling beside her with my hand on her shoulder. "The drive will be dangerous after dark. But if we keep going now, we'll be through the pass by sunset."

"How do you know so damn much about it?"

Mohammed shut off the engine and got out of the car, and then walked a few paces down the road. He stood there smoking a cigarette.

"We don't want to be up here after dark. Let's switch seats, so you're on the inside. I'll tell him to take it slow and easy. You can put your head in my lap and close your eyes."

"Let's just turn around and go back to Marrakesh," she said, still crouching and catching her breath.

"We can't do that."

She looked at me. "Why not?"

Except for her breathing it was dead silent. Enormous shadows were stretching across the black stack mountains and the vast flatness of the valley floor. The sky was blue above but there was no discernible horizon, just gray haze.

I moved my fingertips up and down her back. "Let's go now and get through this part in the daylight. You'll be glad when we wake up tomorrow morning in the Sahara."

Suddenly she stood, shaking her head. Her long blond hair moved over her shoulders. "You're right, Will. I'm sorry. I can be such a wimp sometimes."

She got into the passenger side of the back seat and I closed the door for her, and then I walked around to the other side of the car. The precipice was maybe four feet away.

I took a step toward it.

"Will! Stop fooling around and get in here!"

Far below in the valley shadows the sizes of cities were overtaking the ruined mountains. I ducked into the back seat beside Stacey and closed the door. Mohammed got behind the wheel and started the engine.

"Please go slow during this next part." He smiled and nodded, shifting into first gear and pulling the sedan back onto the road. In the silence the sound of the tires rolling over the gravel was preternaturally loud.

It took fifteen minutes to reach the end of the straightaway. Stacey clenched my hand as Mohammed went slowly around the ninety-degree bend, staying right, close to the rising mountainside. The darkening valley spread farther, massive shadows advancing as the eroded mountains faded into the gloom.

Chapter Eighteen

TWENTY MINUTES LATER we were no longer on the side of the cliff. The road turned up through a series of narrow passes, between walls of rock on either side, dark in the late shadows. And then we were on a high stretch where the mountainside was not as steep, and there were twenty yards of earth between the road and the decline. The sun was dropping behind the mountains and the ridges appeared as nebulous purple layers.

"I'm sorry I was so crazy back there," Stacey said, kissing me. "I feel like an idiot."

Shame spread through my chest. "Some fears are useful," I said, not looking at her. "They keep us alive."

The air was cool now. I looked at her smooth face in the amber gloaming. Tiny shadows of her eyelashes lay like arabesques over the skin below her eyes. I kissed her cheek. Her hair was backlit by orange light, shining blond around the edges and lifting with the breeze that came in through the open windows. The sun slipped farther behind the peaks, hazy strata on the opposite side of the road darker purple before disappearing in black. Endless stars began to appear above and around, drawing us into their silent company.

Inside the car the dashboard lights were coming up as we began the long decline into the pre-Sahara. From her bag

Stacey brought out some cookies with apricot filling, and the three of us shared them, finishing the roll. For a minute the only sound was the grinding hum of the engine and the rush of the wind. The taxi stabbed two long blades of headlight across the empty road.

She looked at me. "Will, how come you don't have a girl-friend?"

I laughed. "I think it's far more remarkable that you don't have a boyfriend."

"Well, I did, in college. His name was Rob. After graduation he got a job in Washington State, and there was no way I was moving there. But I'm asking you."

"I've had a few over the years, but nothing serious."

"C'mon, Will. There must have been someone special for you by now."

I sighed. "It's a sordid tale."

"Tell me."

"All right. When I was seventeen I worked part-time in a bookstore in downtown Chicago, on Wabash Avenue under the 'L' train. I worked behind the hardcover desk, taking care of customers and doing special orders. There was a full-time clerk there named Angela... C'mon, you don't want to hear this."

Stacey slapped my leg. "Tell me."

"She was a couple years older than me, only nineteen or twenty, but already married to her high school sweetheart. Supposedly she fell in love with me. I told myself that I loved her, too, but I guess I really didn't. She was my first."

"You are terrible!"

"I told you that you wouldn't want to hear this."

"It's too late now. Go on."

"After high school I started working at the bookstore full-time. Angela and I were together all day, and then at night we would hang out with her husband and their other friends in their little apartment, getting high and drinking beer. This was when VCRs first started coming out. Suddenly people could watch X-rated movies in the privacy of their own homes."

"Oh, don't tell me!"

"They lived in a basement apartment in this seedy complex on the Northwest Side. At first Angela and Justin said they were born-again Christians, but apparently it didn't stick. Justin seemed to like having me around. I made him laugh. He started renting porno videos at a drugstore near their apartment. He wanted the three of us to watch them together, him and Angela and me. So we did, in their tiny living room late at night. The TV would be the only light in the room. Sometimes he would get up and go to the bedroom by himself, leaving me there with his wife, watching a porno movie."

"Will, you and your friends sound like a bunch of degenerates."

"We were so young... Angela and I started having sex together whenever we got the chance. We would go to my parents' house after my mother left for work in the morning. And then we would ride the 'L' downtown to the store. Sometimes after work we went to motels."

"That is so cheap."

"All the while, Angela and Justin and I were still hanging out together at their apartment, with their other musician and actor friends coming and going. It got to the point where she and I would lay on the couch together right in front of Justin, who was sitting in a chair a few feet away. We would all be watching TV and I would have my arms around her, sometimes with my hands on her thighs. Or he'd be in the next room, and she would whisper to me: *'I'll suck you, and you can explode in my mouth.'* And then we'd go into the bathroom together and lock the door."

"And her husband didn't care?

"I think he liked it."

Stacey guffawed. "C'mon, no one is that weird."

"One Saturday afternoon we're watching a sex tape in their living room. Angela and Justin get up and leave. I figure they're just going to the kitchen to get more beers. I sit there by myself watching this movie for a few minutes, and then I hear them calling me from the bedroom. I find them both naked in the bed, sitting up and covered by a sheet."

Stacey bit her lip. "What did they look like?"

"She had curly red hair, sexy eyes."

"A good body?"

"Yeah."

"And her husband?"

"Just average, I guess. So I walk into the room, and they ask me to join them in the bed. We're all high on weed and beer. I strip to my underwear and get into the bed on Angela's left. She's in the middle, with Justin on her right. The three of us are sitting up with the sheet to our chins, smiling nervously at each other. I slip off my underwear. Justin snaps up the edge of the sheet, creating a bulb of air that moves along underneath it. He says, 'You've got a couple of inches on me there, buddy.'"

Stacey squeezed my leg. *"Will…"*

"So I peek under the billowing sheet and see Angela's naked body. And then her husband pulls the sheet down to our waists. Angela is lying there topless between us. What Justin doesn't know, but maybe suspects, is that I have already fucked his wife a dozen times. But mostly we were having oral sex."

"No one I know has ever done anything like this," Stacey said, her tone more intrigued than judgmental.

"Justin touches Angela's right breast. I hesitate, but then I touch her left breast. So now she's got one man on each of her boobs. She's smiling and closing her eyes, nervous, but you can tell she likes it. And then Justin loses his nerve. 'No, I can't go through with this! When I saw you touch her tit, it changed my mind!' Justin says he needs to clear his head. So he gets out of the bed, puts on his pants and leaves the room, leaving me and his wife naked in bed together."

"What did you do?"

"Angela and I are under the covers. I touch her body and kiss her mouth. She strokes me, and I moan. She giggles and tells me to be quiet. Their apartment is really small. Besides the bedroom there is just a bathroom, a little kitchen and a tiny living room. Justin can walk back into the bedroom at any second. Just then the doorbell rings; it's our friend Alan, a guitar player who Justin forgot he had invited over a couple hours earlier. I jump up and pull on my underwear, and then climb out the window—"

"No!" Stacey yelled, laughing.

"So I'm standing there on the grass outside their apartment window, in my underwear, as cars speed past me on the highway. I can hear Justin and Alan arguing. Justin is saying that he doesn't feel like hanging out after all, and that Alan will have to leave. Finally he does, and I climb back inside through the window and get dressed. And then the three of us go back into the living room to drink more beer."

"So wait, if this guy hadn't lost his nerve, you were going to gangbang his wife with him?"

"I guess so, yeah."

Only her left eye was visible in pale light from the dashboard; Stacey's other half was in shadow. She leaned against me and whispered, *"You would be in her mouth while he was inside her?"*

"Mmm-hmm."

"And then you'd switch?"

"I suppose. Have you ever—"

"No. Never."

We rode along in silence for a few minutes. Except for the headlights on the road the earth was dark. Effulgent stars clustered in the black sky.

"So, what finally happened with these classy friends of yours?"

"Angela turned out to be a nymphomaniac and a pathological liar. She was adopted, and I think the fact that her mother had abandoned her really screwed her up. She started acting crazy, dressing trashy, sleeping with even more guys."

"She was still married?

"If you could call it that. I broke it off with her, but not because of her husband—because of a third guy she'd started up with, Johnny. His girlfriend worked in the bookstore with Angela and me. She was a bimbo, but with a sweet heart. She would giggle and tell us that Johnny had a big one. I think that grabbed Angela's attention. She couldn't wait to suck on it. She told everyone that she'd been accepted into an elite dance troupe and would need to rehearse every night, including on weekends. We even threw a party to congratulate her. But there was never any dance troupe. She was just fucking Johnny. One night Justin caught them in bed together at Johnny's mother's house, and Johnny jumped up and ran after Justin stark naked with his big crank sticking out, yelling 'You're screwing up my life!' at the man whose wife he was banging. But I always felt bad for Justin. He was a little weird, but a good guy, basically. He was a bass player and a singer who dreamed of stardom. He had some talent. He and Angela wound up getting divorced, and he moved to California. Later on I heard that he'd lost one of his feet to diabetes, the poor bastard."

"They both sound crazy," Stacey said. "I think this Johnny saved you from her. But you're much wilder than me. The people I grew up with don't do things like that."

"My friends were always self-centered and nuts, but interesting. But I never really fit in with them, either."

The road was dropping with a long and regular decline into the desert flats. There were no electric lights except the taxi's high-beams shaking over the thin strip of pavement. I rolled the window all the way down and tilted my head to look. The Milky Way spiraled sideways in the center of the firmament.

A long wall ran along the road like an abandoned town barely visible in the darkness. As my eyes adjusted I began to see rows of turbaned figures sitting along its base.

"Look. Do you see those men?"

"What are they doing there in the dark?"

"There's no electricity."

Mohammed was looking straight ahead. The road continued to drop and I could feel the air growing warmer. In the darkness beyond the falling paths of the headlights there were shapes of mud walls and palm groves. We had not seen another vehicle for hours and now there was a single headlight far below, like a warbling star; the luminous point disappeared into a dip in the road and then re-emerged a second later, slightly larger.

"You'll have a completely different perception of this place in the light of the morning," I said. "I think you'll like it here."

She looked at me with one eye visible in the dashboard light. "Why do you always talk like you've been here before?"

The road began to level off as we reached the desert floor. "You see? We've made it."

The light came closer and a motorcycle screeched past us. A minute later there were more headlights, from motorbikes and little French cars, and we began to see boxy houses and stores by the roadside. The pavement intersected dirt alleys that led through slums; concrete walls bordered the paths and intermittent streetlamps threw circles of light on the ground, through which dark figures passed in the distance.

Mohammed swung the car off the road and into a tiny gasoline station. We stayed in the taxi while he got out and filled the tank. The windows were down and the air was hot and dry.

A boy rolled in beside us on a loud motorcycle. He leered at Stacey while he jammed a nozzle into the hole of his dirty red gas tank.

"What's this punk looking at?"

"Ignore him," I said.

Mohammed got back into the car and turned around in his seat to look at me. His face was tired. "This is as far as I go," he said in French.

"I was hoping you would take us to the old Kasbah by the dunes."

He smiled. "I must return to my family."

"All the way back to Marrakesh tonight, over the mountains? It would be safer for you if you stayed the night here."

"I do not think about safe or not safe. If Allah wants me home in my bed tonight, I will be there."

"What's he saying?" Stacey asked.

"He wants to drop us off here and go back to Marrakesh."

"Here?"

She looked around at the strange dark streets. There were no women to be seen. Sulky young men stood in clusters near three taxicabs parked by a concrete square. A few motorcycles and cars buzzed past on the road.

"Fine," Stacey said. "Let's find another ride." She moved to open the door.

"Wait—I have to pay him first."

I reached under my waistband into my money belt and found one hundred dollars' worth of French francs. Mohammed accepted the bills and then got out and took our bags from the trunk. He seemed far less friendly as he sat into the Mercedes and started the engine. We stood there and watched him turn the car around and start back toward the mountains, red taillights vibrating in the dust and dark.

Chapter Nineteen

W E LIFTED OUR BAGS onto our shoulders and then walked toward them. There were maybe a dozen, late teens and early twenties, wearing jeans and summer shirts or light jackets.

"Who's got a free taxi?" I called out.

Three of the young men waved for us to follow them, walking toward their cars at the curb.

"Where are you going?"

"The inn by the dunes."

The others began shouting and waving their arms. Stacey and I walked past them to the first car. With a resentful face the driver looked at me and then at Stacey, his glance lingering on her mouth. Paranoia rushed through me, like somehow this guy knew about Fareed.

We put our bags in the trunk and got into the back seat. The driver started the engine and then suddenly another young man was getting in next to him, in front of me. I saw the dark shape of the back of his head. The others were still shouting as the taxi pulled onto the half-deserted night road through the forlorn town. Streetlamps scattered along the boulevard dropped cups of light onto the gray pavement. Rows of boxy concrete apartments, one- and two-stories high, were set back along either side.

Stacey looked at the newcomer in the front seat and then at me. I smiled and shrugged while reaching with my right hand into my canvas bag on the floor to touch the handle of the automatic. My knees were against the back of the front seat and I gripped the handle of the gun. *She shouldn't be here,* I thought. *Goddamn me for being so selfish and stupid.* But the idea of leaving Stacey sent waves of sick ache through my chest and guts. Within a few minutes the town had faded away and we were on an empty desert road where the only light came from the stars and the headlights that cast long bright spears across the blanched asphalt. Stacey took my left hand and held it in her lap. Air rushed in through the windows, warmer and heavier now. No one spoke and there was just the noise of the wind and the car's failing muffler. The landscape was dark and inscrutable.

We had been riding along for about thirty minutes when the driver turned off the road to the left. The headlights swept a sand-colored wall and then the car stopped. On the edge of darkness three camels were resting on folded legs. A young man in a blue turban and billowing white pants appeared, approaching us just outside the car's beams. Stacey and the driver and I got out. The other boy stayed in the front passenger seat.

"Welcome," the one in the blue turban said in French, smiling and bowing with his hand over his heart.

"Thank you," I said. "Salaam."

"I am Sharim," he said.

"My name is Will, and this is Stacey."

"*Bon soir,*" she said, nodding to him.

The driver set our bags near the wall. I paid him and he got back into the car and drove in reverse to the road, the muffler sputtering loudly as he shifted into first gear and started back for the town.

"This way," Sharim said.

Stacey had her backpack and smaller bag over one shoulder and held my arm with her other hand. We followed the blue turban along the high wall and through a zigzag entrance into a courtyard where candles were burning. In the dull orange light I could discern the shapes of a few umbrella tables and tall potted plants. Sharim led us across the sandy ground to a short arcade at the rear of the courtyard. He stepped through a door and turned on the light; the room had a dirt floor, a narrow bed and a wall fan, a bare light bulb hanging from the ceiling.

"Is okay?" Sharim asked in English. In the glow from the bulb I could see his face clearly—young and smooth brown with a thin moustache and indolent, sexual brown eyes flecked with green. Confidently handsome.

"Oh, sure," Stacey said. "It's fine."

He looked at her with a subtle smirk, and then turned his eyes to me.

"*Tres bien,*" I said.

"Is there a bathroom?" Stacey asked, tossing her bags onto the bed.

Sharim didn't seem to understand.

"*Le cabinet?*" I said.

We followed him out of the room and along the wooden planks under the arcade. In the courtyard an oil lantern on the ground threw amber light across the high walls, casting tall, looming shadows. Sharim picked up the lantern and we followed him through an opening in the wall into a choking odor. I thought Stacey might object, but she said nothing. In the quavering light from the lantern we saw a few primitive sinks along the front wall of the lavatory, and in the back, toilet holes cut into the floor. The methane stink was thick and gagging. Sharim turned and the lantern light swung across showers in the other corner—iron pipes angling down from the wall over drainage slats.

"Just squat, but don't touch the floor," I said. "I'll wait outside for my turn."

Afterwards Sharim showed us around the old Kasbah. A couple of Touareg boys stepped from the shadows, grinning bashfully at Stacey.

"They work in the kitchen."

He led us to the center of the courtyard, into a room with animal skins on the walls. Sharim set the lantern on an octagonal copper tabletop pressed with a Moorish design. There were half a dozen sets of tables and chairs in the little restaurant.

"What do you think of my hotel?" Sharim asked Stacey in French, looking at her.

"He's asking what you think of the place."

She smiled awkwardly. "I'm just a little overwhelmed."

"She likes it very much," I told him.

Sharim's face was proud.

"Tell him I think his turban is beautiful," Stacey said, looking at the golden light playing over iridescent blue silk.

"Wait just one moment," he said, walking a few paces to where another bolt of midnight-blue fabric hung unfurled on a hook.

He stepped over and began wrapping it around Stacey's head. "Oh, no!" she laughed. Within seconds he had finished, and she giggled uneasily as he brought the end of the long piece of silk under her chin, drawing the tip across her neck. Her blond hair shone next to the blue. Sharim led her to a mirror and held up the lantern. I watched her eyes as she saw herself in the glass; I expected to see pride but was surprised by what looked like only slight amusement and embarrassment in Stacey's expression. She seemed to have no idea how good looking she was.

"How do you think they'd like this in Chicago, Will?"

"Every head on Michigan Avenue would turn."

Sharim led us back through the courtyard and up a dark stairwell to the roof, where ramparts stood along the outer perimeter and around the edges of the courtyard. Above and down to the horizon the firmament was endlessly deep, layers of stars drawing us into their infinity. Sharim showed us to the back of the roof where a few mattresses were laid out. "If it is too hot in your room, you can sleep up here in the breeze."

We went back downstairs and Stacey and I sat on a wood bench at one of the tables, with candles burning around us. Sharim had disappeared and we watched the boys light a charcoal brazier and then cook kabobs of some indeterminate meat. Stacey looked at me and candlelight flit across her cheeks.

"This place is so strange, Will. Tell me again: Why are we here?"

"Just wait 'til the morning. Then you'll know."

The meat was smoking over white-hot coals. The odor was not reassuring.

"Are we the only guests here?"

"I haven't seen anyone else," I said.

The boys brought the kabobs and served us. They were maybe thirteen or fourteen, skinny with big feet, and had galloping crushes in their eyes as they stared at her, grinning and fumbling with the plates of food.

"Thank you, boys," Stacey said, not looking at them. "What is this meat, anyway?"

I took a bite and immediately tasted the sourness. "I think it's supposed to be lamb or mutton, but it's gone bad."

Stacey bit into a piece and made a face. I was hungry and forced myself to eat one skewer of the meat and some good flat bread, washed down with warm soda.

We decided to sleep on the roof. We were dressed only in

our underwear and T-shirts, lying on two mattresses pushed together. The night was silent and the stars were white-hot shattered glass.

"Tell me the rest of the story about you and Angela," Stacey said.

"Oh, forget that. It was a long time ago."

She rolled against me and stroked my bare arm. "C'mon, tell me."

"Well, all right... You have to realize that the pain of losing my dad was still fresh."

"You were close to him?"

"Yeah."

"What kind of stuff did you do together?"

"He was a big sports fan, mostly baseball and hockey. We went to Cubs and Blackhawks games. Most of his friends were on the force, and we'd go with the other fathers and sons to an indoor shooting range, where I learned to shoot pistols and rifles. Ya know, people don't expect it from a cop, but he had a great sense of humor. He did impressions that were dead-on, mostly of people we knew. He made me laugh."

We were quiet for a few minutes and lay there looking up at the stars. The sound of the camels grunting and gurgling broke the silence.

"I was in bad shape after he died. I felt like the ground had been pulled out from under my feet, and I was falling. I couldn't even imagine my life without him. I was sad, but also pissed off as hell. For the first time in my life I started having violent thoughts. I got into a few fights at school, mostly ones that I started. For a while I tried to convince myself that I was getting over it, but the truth was that I wasn't even close. That was when I started partying over at Angela and Justin's, and fooling around with her. They made me feel accepted and appreciated, and for a year or two it was fun. But then later, when she started blowing me off for Johnny, I was furious and insanely jealous. Johnny was well-built but dumb as a box of rocks. When I realized what was going on with him and Angela, I started coming unraveled. She denied everything and we were fighting at work, sometimes right in front of the customers. I couldn't stand being around her anymore, so I quit my job at the bookstore and would sit in my room all day. I hadn't started college yet and was drifting. Justin had taken a job on the night shift at a factory, which allowed Angela and Johnny to be together every night. One night I went to Angela and Justin's apartment when I knew she would be getting home from work. It was during the summer and still light out. They lived in this shitty, two-story building on a corner. I was waiting outside for her when I saw Johnny coming down the street.

"'What the fuck are you doing here?'

"Johnny goes into a belligerent stance. 'I don't answer to you,' he says. 'Mind your own damn business.'

"Now I'm really boiling. 'Are you an' Angela havin' an affair?'

"Johnny laughs. 'Don't worry, Will,' he says. 'You've got nothin' to worry about.'

"He starts for her door, but I step in his way. He shoves my shoulder. I flick open a switchblade and watch the fear in Johnny's eyes. I swing my arm sideways and a red line appears across his face."

Stacey raised herself on her elbow and looked at me in the gray starlight. "My God, Will…"

"Johnny brings his fingers to his face and then looks at them. When he sees the blood he's really scared. 'J-J-Jesus, Clark,' he stammers, stepping back from me with his palms up. 'What the hell are we doing? And for a married tramp?'

"And then we hear the sirens. A black-and-white is suddenly on the street in front of us, with its lights spinning around the neighborhood. I throw down the knife and two big cops run over to Johnny and me. I recognize them both. They're friends of the family. The long and short of it is that I didn't go to jail. And I never saw Angela, Johnny or Justin again."

Neither of us spoke. The desert was silent and eternal stars burned in the domed sky, gauzy dustings of light spreading through its heart. In the quiet Stacey and I lay with our bodies pressed together and I felt sleep begin to roll over me. I dreamt of the house I grew up in, a stout red-brick bungalow at Mozart and Berteau on the North Side. When my dad was alive the house was always well maintained. He spent a lot of time working around it and in the small backyard, Cubs game on the radio, and he was proud of our place, especially after growing up in rental apartments himself. Then my dream shifts to after he died: The trim needs painting and the yard is overgrown. The wood of the enclosed back porch peels big rust-colored flakes. I'm sitting with my mother, a blue-collar woman who streaks blond frost on her hair and tries to stay in shape and wear attractive clothes, someone who wants to belong to a higher socioeconomic class, and if she can't then she will at least pride herself on trying to emulate their manners and appearance, even if it means alienating her neighbors and her husband's friends because they sense that she feels superior to them and they know she's no better than they are.

We're sitting in our yellow patio chairs and she says, "You know, Willy, your dad didn't go to that house on a call."

"Whatta you mean?"

"I thought you might have figured it out by now, but I know your version of the story is more acceptable to you." She looks at me and her face becomes Tammy's face, and then Stacey's. Marissa is in the background, half in shadow. "Will, your dad was sleeping with that woman. She didn't shoot him. Her husband did."

Chapter Twenty

I T WAS ABOUT SIX when I woke to the orange rays. The air had stayed warm all night and Stacey was asleep next to me on the thin mattress, wearing just her bra and panties. I sat up and looked around at the old Kasbah, seeing it in the light for the first time. The building was the color of the surrounding sand. In the corner a turret stood another story above the roof; topping the sentinel tower was a white parapet with battlements at its corners, like a square crown, with notches for steadying rifles. White triangles rose at intervals around the sides of the roof. Across the east face of the tower the early sun glowed unchallenged. A bulbous Moorish door cut into the side of the turret had been covered over with plywood, and short wood poles protruded from the mud brick on the sides of the tower. I stood and walked to the parapet along the back edge of the roof. The sun was huge and tremulous, orange and red and just above the horizon. Outlines of the big dunes stood in sharp silhouette. I went to the north side and looked at the light spreading across the flat empty desert. On the far horizon stood dusky shapes of rock mesas. Utterly silent, with a scant breeze. Below camels were sleeping near a well, round and four feet in diameter, with a low stone wall around its mouth and a pointed stump of rock rising from its center.

I put on my pants and shoes and went downstairs. Sha-rim was asleep on a bed under the arcade. I walked past the picnic tables and the long-leafed plants to the lavatory where the stink was thick as I stood over a squat hole and pissed down into the dark cavern below, hearing the liquid slosh against the muck. At the sink I rinsed my hands and face with cold water that trickled from the faucet and then I walked through the courtyard and gate and stood outside looking back at the old fortress, with its sand-colored walls twenty feet high forming a rectangle about half the size of a football field. On the ground the faint delineation of drive-way continued past the inn as a fat white line, curving and then fading into the early glare as it traversed the plain toward the dunes. In the other direction, where the path met the road, a garden with large shrubs was enclosed by a low wall on which there was a hand-painted sign, a child-ish rendering of turbaned men on camels riding past sand dunes and palm trees. Below a couple lines of Arabic script the sign read in French: "*Tomboctou 51 jours.*" I took a few more steps across the rocky ground to see where the road from town led as it continued south past the hotel. The strip of sun-bleached blacktop crossed the flats toward plateaus on the far horizon, the road curving after some unknowable distance behind outcroppings of dark rock. Beyond the road, across the basin, an oasis of date palms stretched for miles. To the west the sky was sharpening to crystalline blue, with no clouds but a trio of thin white parallel lines that looked as though they had been scratched there by God's fingernails. I felt what the French call *le bapteme de la solitude*, the bap-tism of solitude. Standing alone in the vast silence you hear only your heartbeat. A chill ran through me.

Upstairs Stacey was still asleep with her arm over her eyes. Even in unself-conscious repose her body was gor-geously shaped, firm and graceful. Her skin glowed in the early light.

"Stacey," I nudged her bare shoulder. "Hey."

She opened her eyes and immediately shut them against the sunrise, grunting and making a sour face. "Good morning." After a few minutes she stood and walked to the edge of the parapet, seeing the desert in the light for the first time.

"Oh, Will," she said. "Look at this place." I handed Stacey a bottle of water and her blue eyes shone in the light as she drank. She turned and looked around her. "It's so quiet. I don't think anyone else is here except the turban and his boys."

She set the water bottle on top of the parapet and looked at me. Stacey reached behind her back and unfastened her bra, letting it fall to the side. Her breasts were round and high with small pink areolas. She had a tiny waist and curvy hips, and her flesh was golden. Her skin and shape were unbearably desirable. Her blond hair shone over her bare shoulders. She slid off her panties and I removed my clothes. We put our arms around each other and pulled our bodies together, standing naked in the morning sun. I felt my erection press against her abdomen as I ran my hands over her body. *"Sweet Stacey. I wish I had stayed with you in Madrid."*

A HALF HOUR LATER we went downstairs and crossed the courtyard that was half in shadow and half bright in sunlight. A few palm trees were growing inside the courtyard, and as we passed under one the fronds appeared as black spears against the glare. A second later a different angle would reveal vibrant green. We walked around the building of the little restaurant in the center. I noticed Sharim was no longer in his bed, but I didn't see him or the boys.

"It's not quite as bad in the daylight," Stacey said cheerfully as we entered the lavatory. "But whew, does it stink!"

A couple of horizontal slats were cut across the top of the rear wall and sharp planes of sunlight angled down to the floor.

"I'm impressed that you're willing to stay in a place like this. A lot of girls I know wouldn't. Or else they would complain the whole time."

"It doesn't bother me. I'm used to roughing it. We used to go camping with my dad and my uncle, and my cousins." She handed me her toilette kit, wrapped in a cotton towel. "Will you hold this stuff for a minute?"

I walked outside the wall by the camels. They were starting to wake up, and their grunts and gurgles were comically loud through the silence. The flat desert basin stretched out incalculably. In the distance a couple of boys on donkeys were crossing the expanse. They looked less than ten years old and rode sideways on the gray animals, the boys' thin brown legs dusted white and bouncing with the movement. Bundles of sticks were tied on the animals' backs. I could see the image clearly but it was too far away to hear, mute in the desert's visual silence. I had never been farther from my own reality.

Back in the courtyard I saw Stacey standing by the entrance to the lavatory.

"I need my soap and shampoo."

She went inside and a minute later I heard splashing on the floor and the sound of her shrieking under the cold well water. I stepped into the lavatory and saw her over a half-wall partition. Water ran down from a pipe sticking out of the wall. Stacey stood naked on the wooden slats and turned around to wet her hair and body. I watched as she shut off the water and soaped herself and then resumed the cold flow to rinse. I had to admire her. She easily could have been a spoiled brat, but instead was a strong and disciplined young woman. I tossed over her towel and she dried herself, and then she changed into shorts and a top before stepping from behind the divider.

"It's freezing at first," she said, smiling and spirited. "But it feels so good to be clean."

I took my turn and then shaved with the cold water, standing before a wall mirror that was cracked through the center, bifurcating my reflection.

In the courtyard Stacey was sitting on a picnic table, trying to communicate with Sharim. The boys stood near the entrance to the kitchen, their attention welded to her. I wondered if they had seen us on the roof. The expression on Sharim's lean brown face was detached and confident. Full of sexual knowing, his languid gaze caressed her. Stacey seemed not to notice.

"I wish I could understand what you're saying," she said to him. "But I don't speak French or Arabic."

I exchanged greetings with Sharim and then Stacey and I waited while the boys prepared scrambled eggs and served them to us with fresh bread. She drank coffee and I had tea. The boys smiled at her, big-eyed and bashful.

"I think the shorter one is in love with you."

She rolled her eyes and smirked. "I'm sure he acts like this with every girl he sees. Which around here, probably isn't very many."

The food was better than the night before. I looked at my watch and saw it was only eight. Already the air was warm. Sunlight illumined much of the courtyard, glowing on its earthen walls and the sandy ground and the leaves of the potted plants.

"Where did you learn French, Will?"

"High school."

"I studied Spanish in high school and college but haven't had much chance to practice," she said. "I just know a few phrases in French now."

"In college I took a couple years of Spanish, but I had a Haitian roommate who taught me more French, and I practiced it in Paris and the Caribbean."

"Nice lifestyle. You went to all of those places for work?"

"Sometimes for fun."

She looked at me with the same expression I had seen that first morning in Madrid—doubt and determination not to be fooled.

I wanted to tell her that I loved her. But I fought the urge. "I really wish I had stayed with you since Madrid, and never wasted my time with those others."

"We're together now."

"I know, but..."

"But what, Will?"

"Nothing. When we get back to the States, can I visit you in Michigan?"

"Or maybe I'll come to Chicago. I've been there before. After eighth grade we took a class trip and stayed at the Palmer House." She looked at me. "Is there anything wrong, Will?"

"No, I'm all right."

When we had finished eating our breakfasts the boys came and cleared the table, still giggling and gawking at the blond goddess in their midst.

Hey, look," she said. "I guess we're not the only guests here, after all."

A stocky young white guy in a T-shirt and khaki shorts appeared from one of the rooms at the far end of the courtyard.

"Good morning," he said with a British accent as he walked toward us.

"Good morning."

"And may I say, miss, what a lovely sight you are, here in this place."

She cast her eyes down, embarrassed. "Thank you."

"I'm Kenny."

"Stacey. Pleased to meet you."

I introduced myself and shook his hand.

"You got in last night, then?"

"Yeah, just made it over the mountains before dark."

"How long have you been here?" Stacey asked him.

"Three days. We've been stuck here. My friend Ted is sick as a dog."

"What's wrong with him?"

"Puking, the runs, chills, fever. The whole fucking lot— pardon my French."

"You'd better get him to a doctor," Stacey said.

"Around here?"

"How long's he been sick?" I asked.

"Night before last was when it started getting bad."

I remembered the bad meat that we ate. "I have something that will help him."

Kenny looked at me, hopeful but dubious. "Yeah? Like what?"

"A powder that you mix with bottled water, to re-hydrate his body. Also antibiotics and Tylenol."

Stacey seemed taken aback, maybe irritated. "You have all those things, Will?"

"Yeah."

"Maybe you should save them for yourself, in case you get sick."

"It's all right. I've got extras."

"Oh, that will be a big help, Will," Kenny said, his voice animated. "Thank you very much. You always travel like that, mate, so prepared?"

"For the last couple of years."

"Ever since he started working for the agency."

Kenny looked at her blankly.

"She's pulling your leg. I'm a travel writer. Got sick a few times myself, so now I carry these kits."

I asked Sharim for a bottle of mineral water for Ted; he said the boys would bring one and make soup for him. The smaller of the two ran to the kitchen and returned with the bottle of water, nearly tripping over himself as he stared big-eyed at Stacey. She seemed oblivious to his attention. I went to our room and searched inside my duffel bag for the zippered pouch where I kept the powder and the pills.

Kenny walked ahead of us. The door to their room was half open and he stuck his head inside to speak to his friend before waving us over. Stacey stopped short of the door. The air inside was close and hot, and stunk of fever sweat. There were two narrow metal beds.

"Teddy boy, this is Will, from the States."

Ted sat up on the edge of his bed, a skinny twenty-two-year-old Brit, narrow-faced with mussed blond hair and a Public Image Ltd. T-shirt. His face was pale and perspiring.

"How you doin'?" he asked, forcing a smile.

"Hear you're not feeling too well."

"Sick as fuckin' hell." Ted looked at Kenny and chuckled. "Kenny says you're a travel writer."

"Sometimes, yeah."

"So you know how to deal with this, then? I mean, you write articles about it, stuff like that?"

"Did you get any shots before coming here?"

Ted and Kenny laughed. "Fuck no, mate!" Ted's thin young face looked worried. "Is that bad? I mean, what could happen?"

"Typhoid, hepatitis, tetanus."

"Fuckin' 'ell!"

"Don't worry, Ted. I've got some medicine you can take. You'll be back on your feet soon."

"Thanks, man. I'll pay you."

"Nah, just make sure you take all of these pills."

I handed Ted the bottle and he read the label. "That's you, William Clark?"

"Yeah. Also take this packet. Pour the powder into a bottle of water, shake it up until the powder dissolves, and then drink the whole thing. It'll re-hydrate you."

Ted's eyes widened at the white packet, with its authoritative black capital letters. "Christ, mate, where do you get this stuff? Are you in the army?"

Stacey appeared in the doorway. Ted's eyes lit up and he sat straighter. "Good morning," he said, wiping sweat from his forehead. "S'cuse me if I don't shake your hand."

"Here's your water," she said.

He took the bottle and looked at her like she was an angel suddenly appeared in his sickroom, bringing health and the chance for sex and romance.

I opened the bottle of Tylenol and poured out six capsules for Ted. "The boys are supposed to be making soup for you. Eat it while it's hot. Then take a couple of these."

Ted held out his hand and I dropped the pills into his palm. "I don't know what to say, Will ... why you bein' so nice to me, man? Lemme give you some money for all this."

"Don't worry about it. If you're feeling hot and feverish, take a cold shower. Go sit outside in the shade."

"I'll do that. Thanks again." He looked at Stacey and his attraction to her played like pinball lights across his febrile boyish face.

Chapter Twenty-one

Bᴙ ᴍɪᴅ-ᴍᴏʀɴɪɴɢ the air was in the upper nineties with a hot breeze. Stacey and I walked through a passage to a patio outside the rampart wall, surrounded on three sides by a black iron fence. A rectangular swimming pool was filled with thick green water.

There was shade under a small gazebo, and we sat there on a white-tile countertop around its base. Stacey and I leaned against the posts and looked out at the desert. Past the fence ferns with pointed fronds spiked from the sandy earth. Perhaps a mile away or maybe three, the big dunes were blanched in the midday glare. Along the horizon shelves of rock blurred in gray haze.

We sat quietly for a few minutes, looking at each other. I knew I had fallen for her mostly because of her looks, but there was no use fighting it now. She was what I had always wanted.

Outside the ramparts the sun was a body blow. I felt it move through me in waves. The camels stood close to the wall, chewing greens. We went around to the rear of the hotel, past the iron fence behind the swimming pool, between the pointed fronds that reached high as our heads. The rear wall stretched ahead, flat and light brown. Its surface was coarse and I could see fragments of straw mixed with the cumin-colored mud brick. At eye level for a short man there were rectangular holes in the wall every ten feet, one per room, each hole perhaps three inches high and seven inches wide, cut deep through the thickness.

"Look at these strange little windows," Stacey said, running her finger along the inside edge of one of them. She stopped and peered inside. I came beside her and put my arm around her waist, pulling her body against mine as I looked with her into the slot in the wall.

"In the old Kasbah, the men inside could put their rifle barrels through the holes."

"My little know-it-all."

She took off her sunglasses and smirked at me, eyes clear blue and the corners of her lips curling up. Dimples appeared in her cheeks. The smirk faded from her face and her expression became unbearably sweet and naïve.

I kissed her mouth. "Stacey, honey, I love you."

"C'mon, Will…"

I kissed her again. "I do love you, baby. Ever since I first saw you in Madrid."

"Tell me again, Will," she murmured.

"I love you, Stacey Snow."

"Will, I…"

She pulled my shoulders and we fell onto a soft drift of sand between the wall and a cluster of ferns and shrubs. The sun was almost directly overhead now and the sand was hot. We stripped off our clothes and I was on top of her, our skin sliding together with sweat. Her legs were around me and then I was inside her, hard and burning, plunging into her sweetness. We were kissing with our tongues as I made slow love to her. Stacey was whimpering and tossing her head from side to side and then started to cry.

"It's too much, Will," she sobbed. "I can't take it."

I stopped, still inside her. "What's wrong?"

"You can't make love to me like that. It's too emotional. Just fuck me. Fuck me like I mean nothing to you."

"I can't pretend you mean nothing to me."

"Yes, you can. Please."

My body shaded her eyes. I rolled back her hips and penetrated her deeper, and then started pumping her.

"Stacey, I love you so much, my darling girl."

"Fuck me, bad boy."

I was on my knees, holding her calves. We watched it go in and out. We were both moaning; I don't know how loudly. Her breasts were firm and round and shining and they rolled up and down. Physical and emotional ardor pounded through me, nearly deliriously. I glanced up, barely able to focus, and saw the image at the corner of the rampart wall. One of the boys from the kitchen, the shorter one, was crouched twenty feet away with his pants down, watching us and pumping his fist on his erection.

"Shit!" I stopped.

"What is it, Will?" Stacey panted.

"One of those damn boys is watching us and jerking himself off."

She bent back her head and tried to look at him upside-down, and then got up on one elbow and turned. The boy jumped around the corner of the wall.

"I don't care," she said. "C'mon, don't stop now."

"Stacey—"

She pulled me onto her body and started kissing me. Our flesh slid together.

"Is he there?"

I looked up and saw the boy, back in the same place as before, crouched and staring at us with his mouth wide open, masturbating frantically.

"Yeah, he's there."

"Is he naked?"

"He has his pants off."

"He's stroking it?"

"Yeah."

"Call him over here."

"What? Hell no."

She dug her nails into the skin of my shoulder. "C'mon, Will. Call him over here."

I knew it would be a mistake but I waved for the boy to come closer. He looked scared. I waved again. He jumped up and ran toward us, bare feet kicking up sand, wearing only a T-shirt and holding his khaki trousers in one hand. The boy came beside us and fell onto his knees, eyes wide with amazement as he stared at Stacey's beautiful naked body. He looked at me going into her.

She saw his erection and smiled. "Do you like watching us?"

The boy nodded but looked terrified.

"Keep touching yourself. I want to see it."

The boy watched and jerked himself faster. Her mouth was open and her thick pink lips curled back with the sun shining on her straight white teeth. The boy reached over and squeezed her breast. She grabbed his erection and took it in her mouth. The boy groaned and his body shook. He cried out and yanked himself back. I couldn't hold it anymore and pulled myself out of her. Pearl gray puddled on her lips, neck, breasts and abdomen, shining in the light. The boy ran away, holding his pants and rounding the corner of the wall out of our sight. Stacey lifted her hand to shield her eyes from the sun. We started to laugh.

Chapter Twenty-two

"Y<small>OU MUST THINK</small> I'm terrible," she said.

We had showered again and changed our clothes and were sitting under the shade of an umbrella table waiting for the boys to prepare lunch. No one else was around.

"I don't."

"No, I'm sure you do." She gathered up a defiant face. "But I don't feel guilty. Embarrassed maybe, but not guilty."

"You gave him the thrill of his young life, believe me."

She looked at the ground and squinted in the dampened light under the umbrella, and then leaned toward me and spoke just above a whisper. "Will, let's get out of here. I can't stay here now."

"Sure you can. We haven't hiked the big dunes yet."

"How am I going to look at that kid now? And what if he tells What's-His-Turban?"

"No one would believe him."

"Did you hate it?"

The truth was that the connection I had thought we shared did feel cheapened now, but I realized this was an opportunity for us to split apart, for her own good, even though I wanted to stay with her more than anything I had ever wanted before.

"I didn't want to share you with anyone," I said, "but I

understand what it means to open yourself to new experiences when the time is right." I forced myself to chuckle. "You know, something to remember when you're old."

"Oh, Will, I feel like such a fool."

"Did you enjoy it?" My voice was angrier than I wanted to let on. Shame spread down her countenance like a falling shadow. "C'mon, you can admit it."

Her expression feigned defiance. "Actually, yes, I did. I was really excited, really turned on. It felt so ... *primal*."

A breeze picked up and the palm fronds made a dry rustling sound. We were quiet for a few minutes. Stacey was avoiding my eyes. I felt panic at the idea of losing her. I touched her hand. "Will you continue south with me?"

She gave me a playfully suspicious look. "Fifty-one days by camel to Timbuktu?"

"The road ends about seventy miles south of here, past a village called M'hamid, near the Algerian border. Maybe that's my story. You can shoot some pictures. From there, maybe someone's got a jeep, and will give us a ride."

"To where?"

"Algeria."

"After this I want to go back up to Marrakesh again," she said. "I was only there for one night. I'd like to stay a few days and really see it. And then maybe on to Fez."

Over her shoulder I saw the Brits walking toward us from their room.

"How you feeling, Ted?"

He looked better than he had that morning, but still pale. Ted sat next to Stacey at the table, across from me.

"Still draggin' a bit, Will, but gettin' better, I think."

"I hope we won't have to wait long for lunch today," Kenny said, sitting on my left. "Those boys in the kitchen are slow."

Stacey looked away as red bloomed on her cheeks.

"How much longer are you staying here?" I asked.

"There's a bus tomorrow morning at eight o'clock, going back north."

"Over those bloody mountains again," Ted said. He looked at Stacey, eyes full of puppy love.

We heard the sound of a car approaching and then the door closing. A minute later Sharim appeared, dressed in a blue robe and white turban. "Ready for eat lunch?" he asked in broken English.

"Have been for a while," Kenny said.

Sharim went back to the kitchen and then reappeared with the boys, who carried platters of meat kabobs and flat disks of bread. The shorter boy had his head down as he approached us. He lifted his eyes to her with hopeless longing. She did not look at him.

"Have you guys been to M'hamid?" I asked the Brits while the other boy opened bottles of Coke for us.

"To what?"

"The village at the end of the road. The last dot on the map."

"Oh, right. Yeah, I heard about that place. But with Ted in his condition … you thinkin' of going?"

"Yeah, I'd like to see it. There's an oasis outside the town where you can sit on a high dune and look out over the desert."

"It does sound cool," Stacey said.

Ted perked up. "Maybe we should stay one more night, and then head out there ourselves," he said to Kenny.

"Nah, I'm ready to move on. Someplace with a hot shower." Ted was crestfallen. Kenny looked at me. "I'll tell you what, though. I'll bet the guy who runs this place would drive you there for a reasonable price. I've seen him give other people rides from here."

"In fact we're planning to go into town with him later today," I said.

"On the way back have him drop you near the farms. You walk through this village that looks like it's from the Bible."

AFTER LUNCH STACEY AND I lay in the shade reading. I started to doze but my head hurt from the heat. She was beautiful and sexy in her shorts and sleeveless T-shirt. All of the guys were looking at her. I couldn't blame them. I knew I had no more right to her than they did; less, in fact. She seemed either not to notice their glances, or not to take them seriously. Unlike other girls I had known, Stacey did not appear to encourage sexual attention. She didn't realize the power that she had. But she was becoming more sexual, and I was participating in her change. It was a pain/pleasure sensation, like jealous imaginings that turn you on even as they torture you, and you end up jerking off with tears in your eyes. I felt a cold plunge inside knowing she was better off without me.

At about three o'clock we went out to the driveway. Sharim's old Citroen looked like a gray helmet on wheels. His face wore its usual charming challenge, as if he knew a secret. As he pulled the car onto the faded asphalt and started across the basin Stacey's blond hair lifted in the wind through the open windows. Thick ribbons of it flit up into the air, edges burning gold. I could see individual hairs in delicate, quavering silhouettes, amber beads of light moving along their lengths like drops of liquid. The blue of her eyes was alive in the afternoon light and I saw in them an innocent affection that made me feel both euphoric and despondent, in alternating waves.

The edges of the road crumbled into the desert and the earth stretched out, pale brown. Far in the distance the horizon was a long shelf of rock, the rim of a dried sea. We passed huts, small and round and made of mud with thatch roofs, set back from the road. There were no wires or telephone poles. I saw Sharim glance at Stacey in his rearview mirror, smirking with his sensual eyes. She was looking at the rows of palms and I wondered what she was thinking.

Far down the road another vehicle was coming toward us, beginning as a smeared gray dot where the asphalt faded into the background. As it drew nearer a horizontal line of mirage split the image and it danced as though reflected on water.

"Oh, no," Stacey said, leaning close to me. "Here comes my group from yesterday."

I had almost forgotten. The tall bus came into focus as the gap narrowed.

"Will, they're all going to find out what happened."

Sharim turned his head and smiled at us. "Fifteen, maybe twenty new guests," he said in French.

The bus grew larger and more defined as we neared it on the road. It had a big window in front, silver black in the glare. Stacey looked ahead and her eyes were iridescent blue and full of worry. She chewed her lower lip.

"Quickly," Sharim said, "roll up the windows!"

He began driving close to the frayed edge of the asphalt but didn't slow down. The long dark metal of the bus roared past. Brown dust filled the air and pebbles pelted the Citroen, banging on the glass.

"Don't worry about it," I said, close to her. "You don't know those people. You don't owe them a damn thing."

We rolled the windows back down and hot noisy wind again flowed through the car. The road began to rise with the land and there was a wall of green from the oasis on our left. The Citroen lurched as Sharim swung it onto a dirt path. Presently we came between rows of vendor huts in a small market. He stopped the car but kept the engine running. A young man approached and put his hands on the frame of the driver's window, bending his head down to talk to Sharim. They smiled and spoke in Arabic and the man handed Sharim some folded bills; Sharim put a small package into his palm. They waved to one another as he backed the car onto the road and then started driving again toward the town.

"What was that all about?" Stacey whispered.

"Beats me."

Mud-brick structures began to appear by the roadside. Sharim pulled over at a café where three middle-aged men were smoking and drinking tea. He reached across the passenger seat as one of them stood from his chair and walked to the car. They smiled and called to each other. Like the one in the market, the man handed Sharim money and in return Sharim gave him a small wrapped parcel. He saw me looking at him and gave me his self-assured smirk. A few seconds later the Citroen was back on the road and the dry wind through the windows was animating Stacey's hair.

She brought her mouth close to my ear. "Is this guy selling drugs?"

I could see Sharim looking at me in his rearview mirror. I wondered if he understood more English than he wanted us to believe.

"I don't know," I lied.

"We could wind up in jail, for God's sake."

He drove for a few minutes and then stopped in front of a two-story structure. There was an arcade on the first level with arched entrances and heavy wood doors were set back in the shadows. Pottery was lined up on the ground under the arches and rugs hung on the façade.

"There is a store inside," Sharim said. "I will wait here for you."

We got out and walked beneath the arcade. The air smelled damp, mixed with an odor of livestock. Stacey followed me through a pair of open doors into a courtyard. There was a fountain in the center but instead of containing water it was filled with discarded goat parts from the animals that had been brought to market and slaughtered there that morning. A black dust of flies buzzed around the fountain and the stink grew stronger. I thought Stacey would say something but she was quiet as we bent through a low door into the pantry. A woman sat behind a cracked wood counter; behind her shelves were sparsely stocked with packaged goods and snacks. We bought oranges, potato chips, cookies, candy, bottled water and toilet paper.

Stepping out of the tiny store I nearly collided with a man in a turban and djellaba. We stopped and he looked at me intently. His skin was tough and lined. He looked fifty but might have been thirty.

"Pardon, monsieur," I said.

The man continued staring at me, eyes registering surprise and hostility. He didn't move so I stepped around him. I could feel the weight of the automatic in my bag. As Stacey and I passed through the courtyard with its pile of goat parts and then under the arcade to the street I turned to look back at the man. He was still standing there watching us.

"What was that guy's problem?"

"Who knows. Probably just doesn't like outsiders."

As we approached the car we saw another customer leaning in through Sharim's window.

"Look at this shameless crook!" Stacey said. "Right out in the open!"

I stepped ahead of her and opened the door behind Sharim. The man at the window stood up and looked at me. He seemed embarrassed and turned to walk away. Stacey got in and I shut the door for her, and then walked around to the other side.

Sharim smiled at me. His eyes seemed honest now, as if

admitting everything and yet asking to let it slide on his charm. I have to admit he was likeable. We might have been friends.

Kids were shouting. Two boys, twelve or thirteen years old, approached Stacey through the open window. One pushed ahead of the other, coming within inches of her. But he was looking at me.

"Please sir, let me kiss her, just once," he said in English. "She is so beautiful, her hair, her eyes!" He looked at Stacey plaintively. "I will give you three dirhams. Please!"

She began to laugh. "Oh, my God! No, no, I don't think so, sorry. Will, do something!"

"Please sir," the boy pleaded, reaching his fingers toward her but not daring to touch, "let me kiss her just once!" He thrust his neck in through the open window and kissed her fast on the cheek. The boy jumped back with a crooked-toothed grin, hopping and yelling and waving his arms in triumph.

"Has word spread about me already?" she said good-naturedly.

Sharim started the engine and yelled at the boys in Arabic. He shifted into first gear and pulled the Citroen in a U-turn as cumin-colored dust rose in the air. Men standing in the street watched us pass. The one from outside the store was among them.

Within seconds we had reached the edge of the village and the road ahead dipped into the desert basin. Below on the right there was a wide swath of dark green where the oasis spread south. A little truck, too tall for its width, swayed from side to side as it climbed slowly up the incline toward us. Four turbaned men were crowded together in the front seat, and easily a dozen more sat with bundles on the roof.

It appeared that both vehicles would not fit past each other on the road. Sharim pulled to the right and half of the Citroen was in the dirt as the truck rumbled past. He sounded the car's horn and the men yelled and waved.

When we reached the market Sharim turned off the road to the left and stopped in front of the open stalls. We got out and walked to where men were standing behind the plywood counters of their mud huts. Long flanks of raw meat hung on hooks, flies buzzing around and landing on the red sinew and pus-colored fat. One butcher was a tall thin man in a dingy gray robe and tattered turban who swatted flies from the meat with a stick. Sharim spoke to him and pointed across the road toward the oasis and the farms. The man squinted at Stacey and me. He had a transistor radio on his counter and much to my surprise "Under My Thumb" by the Rolling Stones began playing. For me it was a joyous sound. Stacey and I started dancing and the butcher angrily yelled at us to stop.

She took a long drink from a bottle of water and then handed it to me. In the hot dust the water barely seemed to dampen my throat. As we crossed the road I heard Sharim's engine and turned to see the Citroen scuttling back toward the inn.

"What do you think that guy is up to?"

"Probably selling hashish," I said.

"That's what I thought, too. Is it legal here?"

"No, but mostly tolerated for the locals. For tourists it's a different story." She looked at me. "I read about it in The Real Guide," I said.

On the other side of the road, at a right angle to it, there was a wide avenue of sand bordered by thatch fences and profusions of date palms and tall conifer shrubs. Far ahead a woman walked alone in the hot sun, draped in black. It was dead quiet. We hiked along without talking and the only sound was the muffled thumps of our boots in the sand. The bag on my shoulder slipped and I pulled it back up.

The boulevard of sand turned and forked into two paths. We went to the left through an opening, eight feet wide between crumbling walls of mud blocks. Some sections of the walls had fallen away and we could see green in irrigated farm plots divided by rows of date palms. The soft ground became a rutted dirt road. Ahead the path bent gradually farther to the left and the eroded walls rose and fell. The sky was sharp blue and cloudless.

After a few minutes we reached the center of the farming village. Boxy dwellings jumbled one atop the other up a small slope, all the same sandy brown color. The petit skyline collided with half-ruined walls that angled toward it from different directions, a visual cacophony that confused my eyes. The huts had flat roofs with crown points in the corners and each wall was blank except for a small rectangular hole cut in the upper left. Behind the huts squat palms jutted into the sky at odd angles, like ersatz television antennae. Stacey's expression was serene.

We came upon a boy standing against a mud-brick wall. He wore something like a poncho, white with blue vertical stripes. He squinted wearily at me.

"Bon jour."

The boy looked at the ground. A fly was resting on his face. He didn't try to swat it away. His teeth were streaked with brown lines. The boy looked at me like I was the enemy, unaware of the connection that I felt with him.

Stacey and I followed the path between the decaying walls. A man was plodding toward us with a walking stick. He was small and wore a skullcap. The sleeves of his shirt were folded back and his thin arms were covered in dust. Empty burlap bags were slung over his shoulders and hung below his waist. He stopped and looked at us. The wall behind him was taller than he and behind it there was a date palm twice the height of the wall.

With a few agile steps and leaps Stacey was suddenly standing on top of a shorter wall on the other side of the path. She brought out her Nikon and focused on the man, who looked at her uncomfortably but stood still. I heard the shutter fire. The man started walking again and I nodded to him as he passed. He looked away. He seemed very tired.

Stacey shot some more pictures of the strange little skyline. Eroded earthen cubes of the huts and walls were nearly indistinguishable one from the other in the surreal warren. We followed the path to a gap in the wall and stepped through it, walking along a narrow irrigation stream at the end of the rows of crops. The air was cooler here with water running through delicate canals under the shade of the palms. We stopped and Stacey peeled an orange. We sat there looking at each other and ate the fruit. Her eyes were vibrant with health. It was obvious that she had never damaged her body with toxic self-indulgence, unlike most of the people I had known. Stacey winked at me and bit into a big piece of orange. I smiled and leaned over to kiss her, squeezing my arm around her waist. I knew she was too good for me. Maybe that's why I loved her so hard.

After the last vegetable plot there was a row of palm trees and then the oasis yielded to sand. The ground was uneven, in mounds that rolled against each other. We passed ferns high as my chest and stunted palms with fronds half brown. Stacey was behind me and I turned to look back at her. She hiked confidently, coordinated and athletic over the desert terrain, with a half-full pack on her pack.

We reached a clearing before a dune that rose against the blue. Stepping around a patch of scrub we came upon a decomposing mule carcass sprawled grotesquely in the sand. The animal's head and insides were gone but the hollow barrel of its ribcage remained, covered with bristly gray hair.

"Do you think it was attacked by some big cat or something? Do they have those around here?"

"Jackals, maybe," I said. "But probably he just died and vultures ate the carrion."

We continued up the dune and at the crest saw a long wide descent on the other side. The wind-spread sand was mostly empty of vegetation and burning from a full day's sun. I felt the heat through my hiking boots. Here and there a patch of scrub poked through, or a fern or short palm struggled to grow. We started down the long declination toward the old Kasbah in the distance, brown earthen walls of the fortress set amongst a burst of green on the otherwise arid expanse. From this angle the dunes behind it looked incongruously large. The sky was endless and there were no clouds, just open blue growing deeper and acquiring pink and lavender along the eastern horizon. I glanced at Stacey and saw her gazing at the hotel in the distance, expecting her mood to change as she remembered. But the same look of contentment remained in her eyes. As we drew closer to the inn I saw the tour bus parked outside the walls.

Chapter Twenty-three

I N THE LATE-AFTERNOON SHADOWS the courtyard was already growing dark. My eyes took a minute to adjust but straightaway I could hear the voices—people speaking in German and Dutch, and in English with British and Australian accents. A dozen or more tourists were lying about the courtyard, leaning back in chairs or sitting on the soft ground with their backs against the walls. It was still very hot, easily one hundred degrees. Stacey and I walked toward our room through spaces between the people. I looked around for Frank but didn't see him. A couple of masculine-looking girls waved to Stacey.

The taller boy from the kitchen darted past us and a beat later the other boy appeared. He stopped and looked at Stacey with desperate, importuning eyes.

"Please, miss," he whispered in English. "Can I be with you again? Oh miss, I love you so!"

Stacey turned away from him and stepped faster. I followed her into our room and closed the door. She sat on the edge of the bed and took off her boots. With the door closed the air inside had quickly grown hot and thick. We were both quiet for a few minutes and sat looking at each other in the low light.

"What's the matter, Will?"

"Why?"

"I don't know. You seem distant. Is it because of what happened with the boy?"

"Everything is all right."

She moved closer and gave me a searching look. "Is there something you want to tell me?"

An impulse arose within me to tell her everything that had happened—but I fought it back. "I don't want to drag you down."

"How would you do that?"

I could hear voices and laughter in the courtyard, muffled through the thick wood door.

"You could do a lot better than me."

Her blue eyes were darker now in the muted light. "Unless you want to waste what you've been blessed with, you'd better start believing in yourself more," she said, squeezing my leg and kissing me. Her lips still tasted like oranges. I ran my hands over the contours of her body, pulling her against me.

"I love you, Stacey."

"I love you too, Will," she said, placing her open palm on my chest. "My bad boy. I love you, too."

THE SKY WAS TURNING RED and the boys lit candles, casting quicksilver shadows over the high walls. Kenny and Ted were sitting at a table and we joined them. Ted looked around at the newcomers and dropped his voice: *"It's like an alien invasion."*

"The loo is really gonna stink now!" Kenny said. Ted and Stacey laughed.

And then we heard another voice, one with an ugly edge: "Well, look who is here. The two lovers."

It was Frank, suddenly standing over us. Shadows moved

across his face.

"Well hello there, old Frankfurter," Stacey said. "How was your trip over the mountains?"

"It was fine."

"A real white-knuckle ride, huh?"

The German's gaze softened at the sight of the lovely blonde. But a heartbeat later his sour visage reappeared. "There were many interesting geological features in those mountains and canyons," he said. "But I was never scared."

I tried not to look at him. Kenny and Ted also seemed wary of Frank.

"C'mon and have a seat with us," Stacey said. "How was the stop last night?"

Frank sat at the end of the table near her. "You missed it," he said, running his hand back through the part in the center of his brown hair. "We stayed in a village in the Anti-Atlas, where the dwellings are built up a hillside. We slept in tiny rooms rented by the families. It was an incredible experience. You should have been there, like I told you."

"Well, we've been seeing some terrific sights around here, too," Stacey said. "This afternoon we hiked through a farming village in the oasis several kilometers from here."

"Yes, but you did not stay overnight and have the complete experience."

"But we stayed overnight here, Frank," I said. "And that was its own complete experience. I can promise you that."

Stacey kicked my leg under the table.

Frank looked at me and wrinkled his nose in distaste. He cleared his throat. "You said you came down here from Rabat, is that right?"

"Yes."

"The bus driver just told me something very interesting that he heard on his two-way radio."

"Yeah? What was that?"

"A few nights ago in Rabat, the police shot and killed two backpackers. An American girl and an Irishman. Did you not say that you were traveling with an American woman and an Irishman, Mister Reporter?"

Ice dropped through my guts. Stacey turned to me, startled. "Two American girls and one Irish guy, yes," I said, trying to laugh it off. "But it couldn't have been them."

"Did the driver say why they were shot?" Stacey asked Frank.

"They were suspects in a drug killing farther north. They tried to escape from the police."

I saw Sharim standing in the shadows nearby, looking at me. "Tammy is a spoiled heiress, not a gangster," I said. "It couldn't have been them."

"And then in Marrakesh, they found the brother of one of the dead men from the drug murders. He was tied to a tree, beaten half to death." Frank looked at me coldly. "Stacey," he said, "are you going back with the rest of the group tomorrow?"

"I don't think so, Frank." Her tone brightened. "Will and I are collaborating on an article together. I'm shooting the pictures."

The edge fell from Frank's face. He looked hurt. "It would be far better for you to come back on the bus with the group, instead of getting yourself into trouble out here in the desert."

"It's not your business, Frank," I said, hating him even more for being right. And hating myself for what I was doing.

"I can take care of myself," Stacey said. "Don't worry about me."

"You Americans, you are all … you are just … ignorant dilettantes!" He pounded his fist on the table.

"You're a real charming guy, Frank," I said. "I'll bet you're the life of the party back in Heidelberg." Ted and Kenny laughed. "But I'm not pushing Stacey to be my photographer. If she wants to come along, it will be her decision."

"You are making a big mistake, Stacey." Frank went to sit by himself at another table.

AFTER DINNER STACEY BECAME QUIET and reflective. Back in the shadows someone was strumming an acoustic guitar, and I could smell cigarette smoke and hear people talking softly. The candles burned down and the boys from the kitchen replaced them; flames vibrated in the breeze, throwing waves of yellow and orange light and high, undulating shadows. The night sky harbored deep packs of stars, endless and ineffable. After a while Stacey and I said goodnight to Ted and Kenny and then climbed the stairwell to the roof, with the thought of finding a place to sleep outside. But the alfresco dormitory was already full. Up here the sky spread farther, arching from one distant horizon to the other, enclosed as if by a dome and yet limitless. The moon was waxing but still slight and the Milky Way was a great swirling disc of hot light. The air remained warm but there was a stronger breeze now. We stood together by the edge of the parapet and looked out at the black desert.

"Did something happen with you and your friends on this trip?" She turned to me but her eyes were lost in shadow. "Tell me the truth, Will."

Stacey and I were the only ones on this part of the roof. I heard people talking and laughing along the back edge. I was standing close to her but still looking out at the darkness.

"In a little town south of Tangier, we were robbed. There were three of them. One was choking Tammy. I stabbed him in the gut."

"Jesus Christ, Will..."

"He might have died later. I don't know."

"And what about the other two?"

I stood there, saying nothing.

"Will, what happened to the other two guys?"

"I stabbed them, too."

The wind was picking up and the sound whistled in the air. Stacey's features were half obscured in darkness.

"They were hustlers. They talked my traveling companions into getting off the train with them, to go and see some non-existent festival. It was all a scam. They showed us around and then tried to extort us into buying a kilo of hashish for a thousand dollars. And then one of them got Tammy in a chokehold and was threatening to break her neck."

"Why didn't you tell me this before?"

"I didn't want to scare you away."

"And then what happened?"

"We took the overnight train to Rabat, and I saw you at the hotel the next morning. That night when we were leaving town, Tammy and Nigel were a few blocks behind us on a road by the beach. You heard what happened next."

"You let me get involved with you, and you didn't tell me any of this?"

"I had to protect you."

"From what? Are the police after you, too?"

I looked out at the uneven line of the horizon, where the star-filled sky was lighter than the dark earth below it. "I don't think so," I said. "It seemed like they were only looking for Tammy and Nigel. Those two stood out more. But you never know what could happen."

We stood there listening to the wind. "You've got a ticket for that bus," I said. "You've paid for it. In the morning, after you've had a look at the dunes, you should head back north with Frank and the rest of the group."

"Is that what you want?"

"No, but it's the best thing for you."

"What are you going to do?"

"I'm gonna keep going south. To the end of the road."

Stacey turned and crossed her arms, raising her head and shoulders in a shudder as she faced the black vista. "Let me think about it, Will." She walked away into the gloom of the stairwell. A crescendo of laughter rose from the drunken storytellers on the back of the roof.

THE COURTYARD WAS A WARREN OF ORANGE LIGHT and throbbing shadows. Patterns swayed around the edges of the restaurant room in the center. I was walking behind it when I ran into Sharim. He stopped in the waving light.

"Bon soir, ami," he said, smiling with his knowing eyes. Candles on the ground shone up at his face, throwing shadows from his eye sockets over his forehead and turban.

"Hello, Sharim. How is everything?"

"English," he said, forgetting my country, "I saw your woman a few minutes ago. She looked unhappy."

"Homesick. And the middle of the month. You know how it is."

Sharim's eyes told me that he knew I was lying, but his cool air of amusement seemed to offer the same leniency that he had appeared to seek from me earlier.

"Tomorrow afternoon, after the others have gone, will you drive me to M'hamid? I will pay you, of course."

His mouth curled into a half smile. "You want to go there?"

"To the end of the road. And then, maybe, if someone has a jeep, over the desert. I want to keep going."

He turned his head slightly as he looked at me. Orange candlelight wobbled over his features, the shadows undulating. "The drive takes one and a half hours at top speed," he said. "And then all the way back. Lots of petrol."

"I'll pay twice what you pay to fill your tank, plus your fee for the drive."

His grin spread. "Okay, English. The others should be gone in the morning, and then I can drive you to M'Hamid after the midday sleep."

THE DOOR TO THE ROOM WAS CLOSED. I pushed it open slowly. She was lying there in her underwear in the wan glow of the ceiling bulb. The light pulsed weakly with the rhythm of the generator that powered the inn for a few hours each night. Stacey's body didn't move but her eyes turned to see me.

"It's so damn hot in here," she said. "I can't breathe."

"We can keep the door open a little."

"What was it like?" she asked, sitting up in the middle of the cot and putting her arms around her bare knees.

"What was what like?"

"Stabbing someone."

A corrosive feeling gnawed my insides. "You couldn't understand it without having the experience yourself. You'd just judge."

"Don't assume you know what I'm thinking, Will. C'mon, tell me. What did it feel like?"

In my mind's eye I saw the look on Fareed's face when the knife went into him, and remembered how the dagger broke through the thick wall of his flesh and then slid easily into his guts. I remembered the sound of his head hitting the concrete floor when Marissa kicked him over.

"It's like you're being pushed toward a predetermined conclusion, like the ending is already written. You're scared, but you're also pissed off as hell. It's that combination of fear and rage that drives you forward. And then, if you take the advantage, you feel a rush of pride and relief. You feel calm, in control."

"Those lowlife drug dealers got what they deserved, I say."

"I guess."

"But didn't it traumatize you to see your friends shot?"

Shame choked my throat and I said in a thin voice: "It didn't seem real. Nothing here does. You start to doubt reality and believe the illusions."

I got up and turned off the light and then cracked open the door; the breeze accelerated on its way out the little hole in the back wall. Stacey and I lay there in the dark with just a patch of blue starlight on the floor. I was listening to the faint sound of the voices in the courtyard as I floated off to sleep.

Chapter Twenty-four

I N THE MORNING there was a knock on the door. It was still open a couple of inches and I saw Ted standing outside.

"Hey, Ted." I was trying to open my eyes. "What's up?"

"Kenny and me are gettin' ready to go, and we want to say goodbye."

"Okay, thanks. I'll be out there in a minute."

"The Brits are leaving?" Stacey mumbled sleepily.

"The bus must be coming soon. Want to see them off?"

We pulled on our shorts and T-shirts. I checked our hiking boots for scorpions, turning over and shaking both pairs before we put them on.

Outside the sun glared low in the eastern sky but to the west smooth blue spread to infinity. There was a breeze and it felt fresh at this hour, not the hot wind that would huff over the desert by midday. I looked up at the earthen walls of the old Kasbah, the outlines of its Moorish design sharp against the sky. The two butch girls from the bus were asleep in the courtyard, lying close to each other in a shadowy corner. The long gray tour bus sat incongruously alongside the outer ramparts. We walked around it, past the tall shrubs to the barely discernible road. Ted and Kenny were standing there, backpacks at their feet.

"Good morning."

Kenny was short and when he saw Stacey he tried to straighten himself up to his full height. He smiled at her. "Good morning."

"You're looking better, Ted."

"Yeah, much better, thanks." He looked at Stacey.

"You're going back to Marrakesh?" she asked.

"Yeah," Ted said. "And then to Fez for a couple weeks."

I could see her mind working behind her azure eyes. "Fez, huh? Haven't been there yet," she said.

From far down the pale road behind the bluff I saw the shape of the bus begin to appear.

Kenny was standing near her and I could see that he wanted to hug her goodbye. "It was nice meeting you, Stacey."

She smiled back at him, innocent and unself-conscious. In the early light her skin was torturously beautiful. Stacey smirked with embarrassment. "Well, have a good trip," she said, friendly but not flirtatious.

Kenny lurched forward and put his arms around her, pulling her against him in a bear hug.

"Whoa! Okay, okay!" she laughed.

He let go of her with a sheepish expression. The sound of the bus, a low humming grind, gradually became audible.

"Have you decided about goin' to the end of the road yet?" Ted asked me.

"Yeah, later today, after this bus group leaves."

Stacey said nothing and fixed her eyes on the long green oasis in the distance.

"Right, the bus group," Ted said. "Which reminds me: That fuckin' German, Frank. He sure talks a lot of shite."

"Yeah? What now?"

"Last night, after you went upstairs, he kept goin' on about you, trying to tell us a bunch of crap, like that you're not really a newspaper reporter, that you're really some sort of criminal. But we could see it was all shite, that he's just jealous of you and Stacey."

"I think he has a crush on me," I said. They laughed.

"No, but seriously. You better watch out for that one."

"Thanks, Ted. I will."

The sound of the bus grew louder. I could see it more clearly now; unlike the tall air-conditioned hulk sitting outside the walls of the inn this one was smaller, a rattletrap used by the natives. It rumbled toward us down the sandy strip of asphalt, its old body gray with dust. Luggage and boxes and burlap bags were lashed to the roof, and a few turbaned men sat up there amongst the cargo.

"Well, here comes our ride," Ted said. "Thanks again for helpin' me when I was sick, Will." He looked at Stacey and sunbursts appeared in his eyes that were returning to health. "You take good care of our girl, okay?"

I knew I was running out of chances to do the right thing. I almost told him he should take her back north, but instead just said: "You bet, Ted."

Through the open windows I could see old men in turbans inside the bus. It slowed and passed us, stopping a dozen yards down the road. The brakes squealed and bleated. Ted and Kenny, tall and short, thin and stocky, ran to the door with their heavy packs, waving back at us as they climbed aboard. The old transmission made a grinding sound as the driver shifted into first gear and the bus continued down the road. We stood there and watched it diminish from our sight, the sound growing fainter until silence surrounded us again. The sky and earth seemed to expand, rendering us smaller as the edges of the world receded.

"Let's go take a look at those dunes," Stacey said.

The path on the sandy ground from the road to the side of the Kasbah continued its pale trek toward the dunes, soon disappearing in the sun's blanch. It was hard to figure distances out here. Perhaps the dunes were a mile away across the flat dry ground, or maybe three. The sun was low in the sky behind them and their outlines were silhouetted against the platinum glare. Behind us crisp blue spread wide and impenetrable. The only sound I heard was the scuff of our boots on the pebbly ground. My mind flashed back to the fishing village. I reached over and took Stacey's hand, weaving my fingers through hers. She squeezed my palm and we swung our joined arms. She was looking straight ahead but I saw a happy glint in her eyes, crystalline blue in the direct light.

"Is that a tent?"

Far ahead of us the dark shape became visible to the right of the path, which had become nothing more than jeep tracks.

"I'm not sure," I said. "It looks too small."

We continued at the same stride and within a few minutes I could see details of the little shelter. A black tarpaulin was suspended on four poles driven into the ground, creating a small roof over a pair of mats.

"Was someone sleeping here?"

"Maybe nomads stop during the day for some shade."

The dunes appeared to rise higher as we approached them. In the early sun they threw huge shadows toward us, and as we walked into their murk the edge crept to our feet and then up our legs to our waists. The line of shadow was beginning to rise toward our shoulders, the sun now seeming to rest on the crest of the silhouette-darkened dune, when our steps began to incline. The surface was soft. I could feel my boots sink three inches into the sand. The muscles in my legs tightened. Stacey was wearing shorts and a sleeveless top and strode gracefully up the dune, her hair golden fire in the lateral rush of sun. We reached the first crest and the spine of the dune turned to our left; one half glowed in light and the other declined in shadow. On the light side wind patterns in the sand created tiny shadows of their own.

Ours were the morning's first footprints. We hiked down the bright face of the first dune and up the dark half of the next. At the top I stopped abruptly.

"What is it?" she said, coming behind me.

I knelt and peered over the crest at the flat ground below it. "The blue people."

She crouched beside me. "The what?"

Four men in midnight-blue robes, the material light and gauzy, were packing up their previous night's camp. Three were astride camels while the fourth stood folding a wool sleeping mat, the brocade dyed dark blue and red. The men wore turbans of the same wispy fabric as their robes, but a lighter shade of blue. The man standing had pulled his turban off the back of his head and was wearing it as a scarf. He had coarse black hair, with a beard and moustache. He heaved his folded rug onto a pile of others on the back of a camel. The angling sun cast sharp shadows of the men and beasts onto the sand, rough from their steps.

"The blue people," I whispered. "Nomads. They travel through the Sahara. The dye in their clothes comes off on their skin."

"If we ever get stranded out here maybe we can hitch a ride with them," she giggled. Stacey looked at me with her big innocent eyes. We remained crouched there at the crest, watching the caravan as it plodded away through the flat seams between the rolls of sand that stretched toward the broken bluffs.

On our way back to the hotel we saw a few tourists beginning to walk in the other direction toward the dunes. It was eight-thirty in the morning and the sun was already burning hot. Stacey and I passed a bottle of mineral water back and forth to each other. From this point of view the hotel was nearly invisible; the sand-colored structure blended with the desert and the shrubs and palms that surrounded it merged with the long oasis in the distance. We were closer to the old Kasbah when I recognized the pair of British dykes. Everything they were wearing was jet black: T-shirts, shorts, socks and boots, tattoos, contrasting with their pale legs and arms. Their short hair was tainted black. They waved at Stacey as we approached them.

"Good morning," the more stout of the two said, smiling at Stacey.

"Hi, you girls."

"You've just been out to see the dunes, then?" the other one asked. She was thinner and smaller than her companion, and reminded me a little of Marissa.

"Yes, and they're fantastic," Stacey said. "You have to see them."

"Do you have water?"

The stout one looked at me coldly. "We're fine."

"We were wondering what happened with you the other night," the thinner one said to Stacey. She would have been attractive if she only dressed better and let her hair grow. Up close I could see her chestnut roots showing.

"Will, we're going to catch up for a minute, if you want to go on ahead," Stacey said.

"I'll grab a shower."

I was approaching the line of ferns behind the fence for the swimming pool when I saw Frank come out of the hotel and start toward me on the path. The strap of my canvas bag was tight against my shoulder from the weight of the .380 and my skin below it itched in the heat. I could see no one else but Frank. He looked at me and squinted in the sunlight.

With the momentum of my stride I angled toward him and hit him hard in the gut. The punch surprised Frank.

His muscles were not ready and my fist landed straight into his breadbasket. The wind went out of him. He groaned and bent over, staggering backward and crouching on the ground, breathing hard. He began to growl and then sprang at me. But he came too fast and unprepared. I tossed my bag to the side and let him come. He was hunched like a football player and just as he was about to collide with me I jumped left, turned and slugged him in the side of his head. He lost his balance and fell sideways onto the rough ground.

I looked back and saw Stacey talking with the butch Brits farther down the tracks in the sand. They didn't seem to notice Frank and me. He rose on one elbow but was still bent, his movements unbalanced. With all my strength I kicked him in the rear end and his face scraped across the hard dry ground. My shadow crossed him. "Stick your nose in my business again and I'll kill you Frank, you stinking rotten kraut fuck." As I walked back to the hotel I heard him yell "Fuck you!" but the evanescent sound was swallowed by the vast quiet.

Chapter Twenty-five

AFTER A SHOWER and shave I was sitting on a bench under the arcade outside our room. The courtyard was teeming as groups of bus tourists left for hikes to the dunes and others returned. People walked with towels to and from the showers. The boys were serving coffee with breakfasts of croissants and scrambled eggs. Stacey was back from talking with the tough girls and joined me after waiting her turn for a cold shower. Her hair was wet and she looked healthy and glowing in the shadowed light under the arcade. But I could see tension on her face.

"Let's find a table," I said.

She looked at the courtyard and then back at me. "What did you do to Frank, Will? I found him staggering down the path, cursing that you'd attacked him."

"He started berating me again, so I hit him a couple times."

Her eyes grew bigger and she guffawed. "I can't believe you did that, Will!"

"I figured he's leaving in an hour anyway, so this was my last chance."

She stared at me, slowly shaking her head.

"How about you and the lezzies? Did you have to fight them off?"

"Oh, they're not so bad. They were just being friendly."

The three picnic tables were nearly full. Stacey and I sat next to each other across from a blond-haired German who ignored us, studying a map. The taller of the two boys poured coffee, staring at her as she buttered her croissant.

"The bus is leaving after everyone finishes washing up and having their breakfasts," I said. "You should take it."

Laughter burst into the courtyard as a group of Australians returned from their hike.

"Maybe I will," she said, looking at them.

I felt my stomach drop, landing coldly. "This Algeria plan is nuts, I know. I was an asshole to even think about bringing you."

Stacey sat up straight as defiance spread over her face. "If I go somewhere, it's because I want to go there. No one is responsible for me except me."

Someone gasped. Everyone turned to see Frank walk into the courtyard. There was a big bruise on the side of his face near his ear, and long red scratches across his other cheek. He hurried along the base of the wall, avoiding people's eyes, and went straight to his room at the far end of the courtyard.

"Hey, you all right?" an Australian called to him. Frank didn't respond. A few of the tourists turned to look at me.

We sat in silence for a few minutes and they went back to eating their breakfasts. Stacey seemed mortified. "You should go back with the others," I said, just above a whisper. The German glanced up from his map, grimaced, and then resumed studying it.

"I think you're trying to use reverse psychology on me," Stacey said. "You really want me to come."

"I do want you to come with me," I said, "but I know you shouldn't."

AFTER BREAKFAST I WENT BACK to reading under the shade of the arcade. Stacey was behind me in our room, arranging her things. I knew she might be packing to leave, but I didn't go to see. The English girls walked by in their black clothes and tattoos. Most of the tourists had returned from their hikes, showered, eaten and packed to go. Frank returned and sat alone at a table on the far end, with his back to me.

Suddenly Stacey was standing in front of me with her backpack.

"You're making the right decision," I said.

She looked out at the courtyard and saw Frank crossing it toward the exit with his bag. He stopped and stood there for a moment. She waved to him slowly but said nothing. Frank looked at her and then at me, and then he walked out of our sight through the gateway in the wall.

Only a few tourists remained in the courtyard. The others had gone out to the bus, the engine of which ground and grumbled to life, a louder and more mechanized version of the camels. Stacey was sitting with her feet on her backpack, staring at the tips of her boots. I put my arm around her.

A man in a blue shirt and black necktie stepped toward us and began speaking to her in French.

"He says they're ready to leave, and wants to know if you're coming."

She was still staring at her feet. "No."

"Stacey—"

She looked at the driver and said, "No, merci."

The man walked away from us and out of the courtyard, disappearing through the staggered openings where two sections of the high wall overlapped. We sat there listening. Over the rumble of the idling engine came the sound of the bus door shutting, a deflating hydraulic noise, and then the engine revving as the driver backed down the gravel path to the road. Gray-brown dust rose over the rampart wall into the glare of the late-morning sun. We heard the airbrakes whine and whoosh, and the transmission shift into gear. The big vehicle rumbled and hissed as it started down the road away from the inn, back north toward Zagora and the mountains. We listened for several more minutes as the sound diminished, ever fainter until it dissolved into the silence.

THE HOTEL WAS EMPTY AND QUIET. Even Sharim and the boys had disappeared. The sun was directly overhead, the air a dry burn. A small propeller plane buzzed through the sky heading south, the only aircraft we had seen since arriving at the inn. We lay back on the bench under the arcade outside our room and dozed. After a while I woke and saw that Stacey was no longer beside me. I stood and stretched, looking around the courtyard and seeing no one. And then I heard her calling softly to me from inside the room. I stepped into the darkness where only a steep shaft of hot noon light bled from the hole in the back wall. My eyes adjusted and I saw her lying there completely nude, her legs spread and the flesh of her body taut and golden, perfectly shaped. I took off my clothes and crawled onto the cot between her legs. I kissed her body, kissed her everywhere.

LATER WE ATE LUNCH, now as the only guests in the hotel, at a table shaded by an umbrella. The boys had killed and grilled a chicken, which we ate with flat pita bread washed down with bottles of warm Coke. Neither of us mentioned her decision, or appeared even to acknowledge it. I was both happy and ashamed that she had not gone back with the others. Stacey was radiant in the filtered light underneath the umbrella. She gave me a loving look that nearly broke my heart.

The shorter boy brought more bread to the table. This time she did not avoid his eyes. The boy appeared to breathe heavier.

"What's your name?" she asked.

"Ali," the boy said. He looked at her with astonished eyes.

"Ali, I am sure that you will find a beautiful wife someday."

The boy's expression was forlorn. "I don't want you to leave. It's so hard being out here with my brother and cousin, watching people come and go. I'll never see you again." He began to cry, bending over and shielding his eyes with the palms of his hands. Stacey stood and put her arm around him. He threw himself against her, hugging her waist and pressing his face against her chest.

"All right, it's okay," she said, pushing him away gently. His brother called him and Ali averted his eyes as he ran back to the kitchen, sobbing.

AFTER LUNCH STACEY AND I were lying on a hammock under the arcade.

"It is time for your ride."

I opened my eyes and saw Sharim standing over us in a white turban and blue robe, a grin on his tanned face. My arm was around Stacey and she suddenly sat up, making the hammock swing. Sharim looked at her with sly eyes.

Our bags were packed. We used the foul-smelling lavatory one last time. I bought four bottles of drinking water from the hotel and loaded my duffel and Stacey's backpack into the trunk of Sharim's Citroen. We got into the rear seat with our shoulder bags and he backed down the driveway and onto the road, shifting into drive and gunning the engine. Ali was standing by the side where the pavement crumbled, waving to us dejectedly as the car sped past.

She sat in the center of the back seat, and I was on her

right. Sharim was soon doing eighty on the pale narrow road. The windows were all the way down and the wind blew our hair around. After twenty minutes we had passed the green line of palms and the desert spread out a vast basin, dusty gray brown, dark shelves of rock on the far horizon like immense ghosts. A couple of times I caught Sharim glancing at Stacey in his rear-view mirror. But mostly he looked straight ahead, humming happily to himself. He seemed to be enjoying the drive. There were no other vehicles on the road; no houses or towns, no signs.

It felt good to sit close to her, our bodies pressed together. I thought back to our lovemaking in the room, which had been slow and passionate this time. She had not cried. Now we were quiet and watched the strange barrenness flash by in the foreground and shift gradually behind. After forty minutes the road reached a long plateau and Sharim climbed the Citroen up the turning path. At the top Stacey said, "Will, let's stop here and take a picture."

Sharim pulled the car to the side away from the cliff. Stacey and I got out and walked to the edge, a windblown ridge of pulverized rock high as our knees. We looked down at the spreading emptiness. Strange wiggling white lines scratched for miles across the desert floor, eventually lost in remote gray. The sky here was a wan blue, with the air full of dust. My jacket fluttered against me in the wind. Stacey was wearing khaki pants and a white cotton shirt. She took a couple of steps back and focused her camera on me. I tried to smile as I squinted into the sun.

I snapped a couple pictures of her and then we got back into Sharim's car. He was sitting contently behind the wheel, gazing off with a slight smile and smoking a cigarette. I could smell hashish mixed in with the tobacco. He offered it to me and I took a couple of long drags before handing it back to him. Stacey looked at me but didn't say anything.

From the plateau we began a slow decline into a bowl of inscrutable distances. Ruined mountains like stacks of black rock plates, each disk a little smaller than the one below it, stood one here, off to the left, one there, far away to the right. Sandy dust hung in strata around the bases of the old mountains, unwilling to surrender whence it came.

Stacey looked around wide-eyed. She turned and kissed me on the mouth. Her eyes were innocent, free of tough affect. I put my arms around her shoulders and pulled her toward me. I could feel Sharim watching us in the rearview mirror, but I didn't look back at him.

Even as he held the speedometer at one hundred forty-five kilometers per hour, we seemed to progress slowly across the immense flat landscape. The sizes of the ruined mountains barely appeared to change as we sped toward them. In what seemed like delayed increments we eventually overcame and passed the massive black rocks, their shadows turning with our viewpoints.

Below us where the earth declined we could see a checkpoint by the side of the road.

"We are nearing the border," Sharim said. "He will need your passports."

It took fifteen minutes to reach the hut. A white-and-red striped gate was down, blocking us from passing. As we drew nearer I saw a man in uniform standing outside the booth. He smiled when he saw Sharim, who brought the car to a stop. They called to one another in Arabic, talked and laughed. Sharim handed the guard a small package wrapped in white cloth. The man took it and smiled.

"My God," Stacey whispered. "This guy has customers everywhere!"

The guard stepped inside the hut for a moment and then returned, looking at Stacey and me closely for the first time. His congenial expression cooled as his eyes met mine. He wore a .45 on his belt. The man spoke to Sharim in Arabic.

"He wants to know what you are doing here," Sharim said languidly, turning halfway to meet my eyes. "I told him you are tourists staying at my hotel, and that you've come to see the big dunes at the end of the road. Okay?"

"Okay."

The guard looked at us gravely. He took our documents and stepped back inside the hut. When he returned he spoke to Sharim.

"There is a toll to pass here," Sharim said. "Fifty dirhams each way for every car. And then he will stamp your passports."

I had the cash in my pocket and handed the rolled bills through the window to the man. When he returned with our passports he stopped beside the car and stared at me, holding the documents in his hand. I took off my sunglasses and looked back at him. After a pause he handed me the passports and then lifted the gate for the Citroen to pass. Sharim waved to him as he accelerated the car down the empty road.

The pale ribbon of asphalt banked to the southeast and there were stretches of green below. Twenty minutes later Sharim was pulling the car into a wide, sandy square, the center of the village. A long featureless wall of mud brick bordered one side. There were just two doors in the wall, thirty feet apart and made of brown wood, squatting half the height of the wall itself, and a small square window, a foot by a foot. The rest of the wall was blank and nearly colorless, merging with the ground. The square was a big sandbox pocked with camel tracks, and the Citroen slipped as the tires struggled to find traction. At the end of the wall there was a café with three little tables and no awning. Sharim stopped the car. We got out and sat down. He spoke to a heavy man at the next table who slowly looked at Stacey and me with what seemed like tired annoyance. He turned his turgid eyes to Sharim and listened to him talk. When he looked back at us the man's expression was more alert.

"What you like for drink?" Sharim said.

"He speaks English?" Stacey looked at me.

"Do you?" I asked him.

Sharim grinned. "Just some little."

A thin old man appeared and greeted us. We ordered pastries and carbonated mineral water. On the other side of the sandy square the tree line of the oasis rose with the dunes.

"You should be writing about this place for National Geographic, Will."

"You're right, I should."

Stacey smiled and removed the lens cap from her Nikon. She brought the viewfinder to her eye and closed the other; lashes swept down over her skin. "There's one for your article."

We refreshed ourselves with the cool bubbly water. As we stood to leave Sharim again spoke to the fat man, whose face hung in sweaty, unshaven rolls. Stacey and I got back into the Citroen and Sharim spun the tires in the loose sand before they grabbed hold and the car jumped forward to the thin band of pavement. He hit the gas.

"The man has a nephew with a jeep who can take you farther into the desert," Sharim called back to me over his shoulder in French. "He will drive out and meet us in a little while. All right?"

"Why don't you just say it in English?" Stacey asked him with an irritated face. Sharim said nothing and continued driving. There were tall palms on either side of the road now. Long shadows crossed the pavement and sunlight flashed between them.

"I think he only knows a few words and phrases."

"What was he saying?"

"The man's nephew is coming with a jeep to drive us into

Algeria."

"Jesus, Will. Don't go. Come back with me."

"Let's just take a look at the jeep and the driver. If they seem all right, maybe you can still come with me."

"Well, American, here it is," Sharim said. "The place where the road ends."

He slowed the car and stopped. Ahead of us the strip of asphalt terminated in a mound of sand and date palms. Sharim turned off the engine and it shuddered before going quiet. We got out and stood there looking around. The ground was striped with long shadows. I walked over and looked more closely at the road's terminus in the earth. The sand seemed to have swallowed the road.

We hoisted our small bags over our shoulders and followed Sharim between two trees into a clearing. On either side there were walls of ferns and palms, the ferns fifteen feet high and the palms twenty-five, the masses of fronds green dividers against the blue.

Ahead of us three square towers made of bricks stood next to each other like chimneys in the sand, twenty feet tall. Each tower had a crude hole cut into its base. Rising from behind them was an entire palm tree that had been chopped down, whittled bare and then re-erected like a giant stick, climbing crookedly into the sky.

"Sharim says it's a well."

We started up the side of the dune. Palms stood at the base and poked up behind the crest. Late-afternoon shadows curved over the sand, the shapes of the trunks and fronds sharply defined against the bright rippled surface. At the peak we stopped and looked down the other side, seeing our own shadows on a lower ridge, crisply delineated and retaining scale and proportion. I glanced at Sharim. His expression was placid as he looked at me, his white turban spilling in a loop under his chin and onto the top of his cobalt-blue robe. Beyond the ridge where our shadows fell there was a clearing where a donkey stood unmoving in the direct light. The animal seemed to be looking at us and appeared small at this distance.

We hiked the crest of the dune and came to a place where we could see beyond the oasis, out over the vast emptiness. There were a few palms in the foreground but then nothing but sand, rolling away in lower dunes toward the horizon.

Sharim rested on the soft crest, gazing at the view. Stacey and I sat a few feet away from him.

"Come with me to Algeria," I said to her quietly, pointing at the landscape. "It's right over there."

She looked at me and the nearly horizontal light, turning amber now, glowed on her face. I saw the mischievous spark in her eyes that I had come to love.

Through the quiet stillness I could hear, faintly at first but growing louder, the sound of a motorcycle engine. The noise intensified as it drew nearer, out of place with the tranquil surroundings.

"What is that?" Stacey said.

The engine screamed and then stopped. We were sitting where two high dunes intersected, and Sharim stood and looked past us down the side where the line of palms rose at the base, shadows undulating toward us over the sand.

We heard a voice call out. Sharim yelled in response. Squinting into the low sun I saw the shape of a young man coming toward the dune. I couldn't see his face but he seemed familiar.

"If this is the driver, where's his jeep?" Stacey asked.

"Tell me, American," Sharim said in English. "Why did you come to the fishing village to slaughter our men?"

Stacey moved closer to me and squeezed my arm.

The stranger started up the side of the dune, coming toward us at an angle. He was a dark outline against the lateral rays and silver burned his edges. And then, as the sun reflected off the sand onto his face, I recognized him as the one with the birthmark on his cheek. He was holding a revolver.

I spun and lunged for my bag. Sand flew into the air. I opened the fasteners and reached into the bottom, grabbing the Walther. Stacey's eyes swelled with fear as she saw the pistol in my hand.

"Stacey," I yelled, "run down the other side!"

The man raised his gun. A bullet ripped the air beside my head. Stepping forward I aimed the .380 and fired—but missed. He jumped but continued up the dune, leveling his weapon at me again.

Stacey screamed: *"WILL!"*

I turned to see Sharim standing behind her with his left arm around her chest, holding the jagged blade of a hunting knife against her neck. The sun shone on her terrified blue eyes and glared off the dagger.

Another shot whipped past me. The stranger stood against the horizontal light. I aimed the automatic as he raised the revolver again. For a moment time seemed to stop; I thought of my father and waited for the bullet to pierce my heart. Stacey screamed. I fired. The man's head jerked and blood curved in a high arc through the empty air over the slope of the dune. His legs took another half step forward and then he fell to one side and rolled down the hill.

"Throw the gun to me. Or I will do the same to her that you did to my friends."

Stacey's mouth was open and her chest was moving up and down. Looking Sharim in the eye I slid the safety back with my thumb and threw the gun to him. It landed with a thud near his feet.

He pushed her to the side and reached for the pistol. I dove to where the stranger had fallen. The long shadow of a date palm fell across him but a trail of his blood shone red in the light. My heart was pounding. Sharim was standing over me at the peak of the dune against the cloudless sky, sun bright on his blue robe and white turban. He aimed the .380 at me and tried to squeeze the trigger. A second later I saw the gray metal of the revolver in the sand beside me.

"If I can make it back to Madrid I'll be paid forty-thousand dollars for killing Fareed. And twenty thousand more for killing you."

"Van Beek will never pay. He will have you murdered, too."

My first shot hit him in the collarbone. I heard it crack. Climbing the dune I fired three more times, missing once and hitting him in the chest and below his left eye. A strand of his turban flew back behind his head, red with blood. He staggered and fell, his body sliding backwards a few feet down the dune before coming to a stop as his head and shoulders dug into the sand.

Stacey sank to her knees and her face went white. Blood bloomed in the center of her white cotton shirt and she fell forward. My insides turned to ice water and I felt my spirit leave.

The desert spreads silently, patterns of light and shadow blurring as they repeat into the distance. In another hour the Sahara and sky will turn red and then black. Shadows will consume the earth and the stars will emerge once again, pulling me up and apart, ever farther into their shattered infinity.

ABOUT THE AUTHOR

Gregory W. Beaubien has written hundreds of feature articles for publications including the *Los Angeles Times*, the *Chicago Tribune*, *Audubon*, and *Travel + Leisure*, reporting from Europe, North Africa, Southeast Asia, Central America, South America, the Caribbean, and the United States. *Shadows the Sizes of Cities* is his first novel. He lives in Chicago with his wife and daughter. The family also spends time in Lima, Peru.